CRAZY EIGHTS

CRAZY EIGHTS

Barbara Dana

HARPER & ROW, PUBLISHERS
NEW YORK, HAGERSTOWN, SAN FRANCISCO, LONDON

Crazy Eights

 Printed in the United States of America. For information address Harper & Row, Publishers, Inc., 10 East 53rd Street, New York, N.Y. 10022. Published simultaneously in Canada by Fitzhenry & Whiteside Limited, Toronto.

FIRST EDITION

Library of Congress Cataloging in Publication Data
Dana, Barbara.
Crazy eights.

SUMMARY: Fourteen-year-old Thelma fights to recognize and maintain her own identity.
[1. Identity—Fiction.] I. Title.
PZ7.D188Cr [Fic] 77-25645
ISBN 0-06-021388-4
ISBN 0-06-021389-2 lib. bdg.

I

To my mother and father

I would like to thank my beloved Guru, Hari,
and my beloved Paramguru, Ralph Harris Houston.
Without their help this story could not have been written.

—B.D.

NORTH WOODS SCHOOL

When the shrink up here first talked to me about writing I thought he needed help.

"It appears to me you've been reluctant to verbalize your feelings here lately."

I'll say. Who wants you poking around in my brains? Give them an inch they'll take a yard.

"It occurs to me that perhaps jotting down some of the experiences you feel were responsible for bringing you here might help us."

Screw you.

"What do you think?"

"I don't know."

"It's worth a try."

About a month later when I hadn't "jotted down" (I hate that phrase) one word he brought it up again.

"Have you given any more thought to jotting down some of those early experiences?"

"No."

"I'd like you to."

What? A demand?! Not from you!

Anyway, he FORCED ME to write one sentence a day which for reason of propriety I won't quote here. Strange as it seems though I started getting with it. After a few weeks I was writing paragraphs filled with hate and vengeance. Fun. I won't include those either. I'll begin with the stuff that approaches decency. There came a point when I couldn't stop writing. There, I think, it begins to be interesting. I don't know. I hope so. Anyway, here it is.

—T.B.

CRAZY EIGHTS

THE END

CHAPTER ONE

It wasn't smart to set fire to Ethical Culture. If I'd been thinking in those days I never would have done it. Well, I was thinking. I was thinking too much. An endless tape spinning in my head, speeding up, faster and faster. Meditating has slowed that down, thank God, but I'm getting ahead of myself.

I'm sitting in the rec room up here in the northern wilderness. North Woods School, a sort of subtle reform school but not a bad place as it turns out. I owe a lot to this place.

My family lives in Maplewood, New Jersey. I don't live there anymore which is fine with me. I mean it's a perfectly nice place if you like perfectly nice places. I don't. Also, I don't like my family.

First, and foremost, there's my mother. She's truly a bitch. She's a very strong lady. She wants to be in control, to boss, to dominate, to push around. That's about all she likes, squelching and bossing. That and having coffee with "the girls." "The girls" are not really girls at all. They are housewives (married to houses?), women the average age of which is thirty-five. Anyway, they call themselves girls and they sit around in the morning and drink coffee and talk about whichever girls couldn't make it for coffee that particular morning. They talk about these absent ones and the husbands and children of these absent ones and sometimes even about the husbands and children of girls present. They sometimes also talk about tennis (however my mother doesn't play) and exercise classes in Teaneck which they're all thinking of taking, but never do. Throw in a few recommendations for pediatricians, landscape gardeners and alternate Thursday girls (maids to be shared on various Thursdays) and you've got the picture. That's my mother's life.

Moving right along now, we have my father. He is vague. I should capitalize that. VAGUE. He lives there and all, but I don't know where he is really. Every day he gets on the train and goes to Teaneck where he's in market research for a paper products company. O.K., I can accept that. A dumb job, but it pays the rent, his purpose in life, I suppose.

Next we have Jennifer. Jennifer is my GORGEOUS older sister. It was in her behalf that I set fire to Ethical Culture. Jennifer is eight years older than me, twenty-two as I write this. She just got married, against my better judgment, to Kevin, a law student from Columbia (the university, not the coffee plantation). They got married at Ethical Culture which is why I set fire to it, but more of that later.

Last of all there's me. I'm fourteen. I'm not gorgeous. In fact, I hate the way I look. My hair is thin, brown and stringy. (Jennifer's is long, blond and thick.) My nose is a little big. My eyes are big, too, which is good, my best feature. My hands are big, which is not good.

There's a lot to say about being fourteen. I believe everyone is born with all kinds of abilities and talents and ideas and knowing, babies, I mean. Babies may know everything. But babies can't do anything about it. They just lie around and cry and sleep and eat and mess up their diapers. They have all this talent inside them, but their motor abilities are so undeveloped that they can't do anything about it. They can't form the words and make their hands go the way they want them to. They have no means to get this inner knowledge out. So they wait for the rest of themselves to catch up. Now fourteen, the end of the second seven-year cycle, it seems like that's the time they can physically express themselves. Now they can be out with all this stuff that was locked inside BUT, here's the big thing, the shield comes down! "Society doesn't think it's right!" "Whoever heard of that?" "That's not the way they want you to do it!" "That's a new idea, it hasn't been done that way, there must be something wrong with it or someone would have done it before, who do you thing you are?" Fears, society, family. Into the compression chamber. Shrivel up and die. Limit the possibilities of everything to the answers already found. I've noticed that most people go crazy at fourteen and I think that's why. They're fighting that shield coming down. Most of them lose. It's a bitch.

CHAPTER TWO

I'm going to start my actual story with the Tuesday Jennifer came home with all the silver bowls. There were seven to be exact.

It was early in October, a cold day. I had my jean jacket on with the strawberry patch and I remember freezing when I got off the school bus. I used to get off at South Coconut and Pinetree Road, three blocks from my house. There are no pine trees on Pinetree Road. No coconuts on South Coconut either.

Anyway, along with Tina Spearer, Tony Trancus, Scott Smith, Myna Washington and Cookie Cushman, I moved along the cul-de-sac, or dead end, as the sign so aptly states, toward my house. All the houses are the same there. Some architect got a bad idea and kept repeating it. The houses are cheap to build. They fall apart so quickly they must be cheap. No trees grow around there, at least not many. Spindly shrubs, some grass, but hardly any trees. It looks like everything is new there, freshly planted, but the development is eleven years old, time enough for things to grow. But nothing grows there. Especially people.

It was paper pickup day and stacks of newspapers were in front of each house. They were all tied with twine, all the same size bundles. Everyone must read the same amount on Pinetree Road, or at least they order the same daily ration of printed matter from the newspaper folk. I guess some read it, some don't.

Bless my dog, Jimmy. He was the only friend I had in the world until I came up here. I miss him so much. He spotted me at the corner of Pinetree and Bayberry Lane (no bayberries) and came running. He has his special shortcuts. He was now taking his Meeting-Thelma-When-She-Comes-Home-From-School Shortcut. That one goes diagonally across the Butterworths' front lawn, through the rear corner of the Vincents' garden (to the great displeasure of Terry Vincent whose zinnias were directly in the line of fire), then across the front of the Smith property. Jimmy then reached Bayberry Lane and me. He leaped up on me, putting his front paws on my chest and wagging the whole rear half of himself, then he licked my face and moaned.

"Down, Jimmy. I love you. Down."

Jimmy is part collie and part setter, or spaniel, or something. Sometimes I think he's a person with a dog costume on, but there's nothing he can do. He's black and tan and white with kind of raggedy, floppy ears and a sad expression. I think he's beautiful. I hope he's all right now, with me up here at school. I know they feed him, but that's probably all they do. I'm sure they never talk to him or play with him or hug him tight like I did. My mother doesn't allow him in the house. They got him so nobody would rob us. They make him stay in the garage. I miss him and I know he misses me. He's the one I want to see, but they won't bring him. I asked them to and my mother wrote it was time I grew up.

So, Tina Spearer and Tony Trancus made a right on Bayberry Lane, Scott Smith (a mean kid) started up his front walk, Myna Washington turned and ran back to the bus stop (for reasons unclear) and Cookie Cushman sat down by the side of the road and took off her shoe. There was a pebble in it. None of us said good-bye to each other. We don't get along. Except for Tina and Tony, but their thing didn't last.

I crossed Bayberry Lane with Jimmy (James for short) close by my side.

"Good dog, Jimmy. Good dog."

There was a large stick on the ground and I picked it up and threw it. Jimmy loves to go after sticks. He brought it back to me right away, but as usual, refused to give it up. I love that dog.

"See you later, Jim," I said when I reached my front door. I patted him on the head. "I'll bring you a cookie."

I let the screen door slam shut and dropped my schoolbooks in a heap on the floor. I don't know why I brought them home. I never did homework. I had a friend in third grade who summed up my feelings. Her name was Nancy Ruber. She had black curly hair which she wore in pigtails. Her aunt asked her once if she had done the assignment in her workbook. Nancy said, "No."

"Why not?" asked her aunt.

"Who wants to plow through three hundred and sixty-five pages of crap?"

Right on, Nancy. She was eight, but she had it together.

I went into the kitchen, always impeccably clean, but never

any good smells coming from it. My mother feels cleaning is more important than cooking. Cooking is an afterthought. When the cleaning gets done whatever time is left, she cooks something. Something plastic and tiny, without odor or taste. I opened the bread box and took out a rectangular Entenmann's chocolate cake. My father and I love chocolate. I'm glad I have a fellow chocolate fan. My mother would never buy it for just me.

I poured myself a glass of milk and took the milk and cake into the living room. I'm not allowed to eat there, but nobody else was home. Everyone else in the family is allowed to eat in the living room. Also any strangers that come to the house are allowed to eat in the living room. I've never figured all that out.

I remembered Jimmy and got him a cookie, an Oreo. He loves Oreos, but he's not choosy. Any cookie will do. I opened the screen door. He was sitting on the front step, waiting for his cookie. He would have waited till nightfall. Dogs are something else. I gave him the cookie and let the door slam again. Then I put on a record—Stevie Wonder—and returned to my cake. That's when Jennifer came in with the silver bowls. She banged first on the door, asking for help. She plays a helpless game.

"Hello. . . . Anyone home?"

I said nothing, hoping she'd go away.

"Thelma! Where are you?" (She knew I was home from the music. No one else in my family likes music although Jennifer sometimes plays The Carpenters and *Robert Goulet Sings Your Favorites From Camelot.*) "Thelma!"

I put down my fork and went to the door.

"Help me, Thelma. Open the door." She stood behind the

screen holding seven silver bowls, two cardboard boxes, a shopping bag and a large stuffed rabbit.

"You have so many silver bowls," I said, making no move to help her. "What will you do with so many bowls?"

"Never mind," she said. "Just never mind the bowls. Open the door."

"Can I help you?" I asked, still not moving to help.

"Don't be funny, just open the door."

I opened the door and she came in, stumbling over my schoolbooks.

"Why don't you move your damn books?" she said. "You're such a slob."

"Where'd you get all that stuff?" I asked.

"Help me, will you?" she said. She handed me the rabbit. "And turn down that music. I don't know why you're not deaf."

"What is all this?"

"Bev Trussman gave me a party."

"Why?"

"What?"

"Why did she do that?"

"I'm getting married next month, remember?"

"I remember." I set down the rabbit and returned to my cake. Jennifer turned down Stevie Wonder. I could hardly hear him. "Is Bev the one with the rash and the asthma and the husband who's a dentist?"

"Don't be cruel," said Jennifer.

"I'm just asking."

She collapsed in the Early American upholstered chair by the fireplace (nonfunctional, but mother sets imitation red coals with movable lights inside at Christmastime).

"So what's all the stuff?"

"My presents."

"Why did you get a stuffed rabbit?"

"It was a joke." Jennifer took off her beige pumps (I hate pumps. They actually mash the toes together inside the tip) and stretched out her long (and beautiful) legs. She wriggled her toes and they made little crunching noises. Jennifer's feet are now mildly deformed from years of wearing stylish footwear. My mother's feet are seriously deformed. Trends, fashion, keep in step even if it means you can't walk!

"What was so funny about it?"

"What?"

"What was the humorous aspect to receiving the rabbit?"

"I don't know," she said. "It's not important."

"The joke was wasted on you, I guess."

"I guess it was."

"What will you do with so many silver bowls?"

"Leave me alone!" said Jennifer, suddenly turning nasty. "Take your cake and get out of here. You know you're not allowed to eat in the living room."

But the silver bowls had great significance to me. I had to explain.

"No, wait, Jennifer," I said. "The thing about these bowls is—"

"Would you mind?" she interrupted me.

"Hear me out. O.K., you were given these seven silver bowls but there's no way you can use them. You've got too many. But time, precious time, must now be spent. First, thank the people for these bowls you don't want and don't need. That's only polite. But that means buying the stationery, stamps and a pen to write with. You write your seven notes, you mail your seven notes, but that's not all. You now have care and maintenance. Polish and shine these bowls you don't need and don't want. That means getting the money to buy the polish and the rag, and setting aside the time and energy to do the polishing.

"Jennifer, it's not just the bowls. You do this all the time. All your energy goes into taking care of things you don't like, don't want and don't need. You don't have time for anything else. There's another step I forgot. THE PARTY FOR BEV. That's only polite and the bowl or whatever thing you give Bev in return for her thoughtful bowl. You give Bev something she doesn't want or need, and then she has to take care of that. It's like a chain letter, spreading wasted energy. Why not just say something like—'Bev and everybody, thank you for the silver bowls. It was very kind of you to give me these bowls. They're attractive' (assuming you thought they were) 'but I don't see how I can possibly use so many attractive silver bowls. Please understand if I exchange six of them for something I want, or need.'

"But, no, you take the easy way out and say you've always wanted seven silver bowls and you're stuck with them for life or until there's a fire or some child comes and melts crayons in them. Don't you see the emptiness? Don't you see how you've turned into Mom? You're hollow, just copying people who don't know who they are. Don't you want to bust through? You've shriveled and died inside your idea of yourself like a rotten walnut in its shell."

Jennifer's eyes were closed. She had gone to sleep. I took the remnants of my cake (I love that word, *remnants*. Some words can cheer me up and that's one of them). Anyway, I took the remnants of my cake and went into my room, leaving Jennifer, my empty milk glass, the silver bowls and the stuffed rabbit to fend for themselves.

CHAPTER THREE

My room was always a mess. Jennifer was right in calling me a slob. I stepped over the heaps of clothes, magazines (*Photoplay*, God help me, and *National Lampoon* mostly) broken odds and ends, etc., set down my cake and flopped, facedown on my bed. My life was a mess, a failure. I hated myself. I was miserable at school. I had no one I could talk to. There was Penny, but she was so happy, so enthusiastic, I thought she was dumb (I've come to believe differently). She was (she still is, but I don't see her up here at NWS so she has slipped into the past tense), anyway, she was one of five children in a family with not too much money. She was always busy—school, baby-sitting, a paper route, caring for her two guinea pigs, one hamster, two cats and a praying mantis (who has since died), ballroom dancing, school trips, watching T.V., reading magazines, bike riding (something I enjoy), baking cookies, reading stories about witches, buying clothes, going to the movies and helping her mother clean the house. She seemed to enjoy it all. She was kind, but I mistrusted her. We had little in common. Most of the other girls around Maplewood I loathed. Apprenticing to be like their mothers. Some of the boys had more imagination, more daring. Jonathan Bessmer and I sometimes would ride our bikes over to Parkway Gardens, a two-story garden apartment setup, with long driveways running lengthwise at each side. There were garages on the ground floor, and above them terraces. Across the driveways was a long row of hedges. We used to ride our bikes over there and then hide in the bushes and throw light bulbs onto the terraces across the driveway. I'm not proud of that. Once somebody recognized me and called my house. It was a Sunday and my father came to get me. He didn't say anything except that they called and I should go home. Then he went away. At dinner that night he didn't talk to me, but he didn't talk to anyone else either so maybe he was upset about something else. My mother made me wash the kitchen floor every day for a week because of those light bulbs. I didn't eat much that week.

Anyway, there I was lying facedown on my bed feeling sorry for myself. What was there to look forward to? Silver bowls and thank you notes? Not having to go to school? THAT'S NOT GOOD ENOUGH! I had a longing to do something great, something important, something with meaning, but what? I couldn't even manage to make my bed in the morning, or comb my hair, or sit through a meal without wanting to jump up and strangle my mother. Is this someone destined for greatness?

"Thelma."

My mother was knocking at the door.

"Thelma!"

"Yes?"

"Your books are in a heap in the hallway. Move them, please."

"All right."

"Have you begun your homework?"

"No."

"Better get to it. In a half hour I want you to set the table."

"What are we having?"

"Codfish cakes."

I got up and lit some incense. My mother hates the smell, but I really don't think that's why I like it. It relaxes me. It gives me a feeling of possibility.

The codfish cakes were awful. They were frozen, or had been until about twenty minutes before we ate them. My father stared at his fish cake and seemed to go into a trance.

"Something wrong with your food?" my mother asked. My father didn't seem to hear. "Is there something wrong with your food?" my mother asked again, louder this time.

"What?" My father seemed startled. "Oh, no. I was just wondering what it was."

My father's sweet, but he's in a world of his own.

"What we have is a fishcake," my mother said.

"Codfish, isn't it, Mother?" put in Jennifer. Such a dear.

"Yes, cod."

"It's like a rock," I said. "I hate this fishcake."

"How was school today, Thelma?" asked my mother.

"It stank."

"We can't always do as we'd like," said Mother.

So it would appear.

"What troubled you about school today, Thelma?" asked

my father. He had cut into his fishcake and was staring at it with a confused look.

"Everything," I said.

"Oh dear!" said my father. I think he was referring to his fish.

I remember that day as your average horrible day at school. I started by failing a Latin test. (*Amo, amas, amat.*) I mean, WHY STUDY LATIN? I refused to take it up here at NWS and they said O.K., thank God! Months of boredom declining bizarre combinations of sounds, dead letters. And what do you get? If you don't want to be a priest, what's left for you? I guess you could teach it to other people who don't want to know the language. Oh yes! The most important thing! A knowledge of Latin helps you get into the best colleges (assuming that's where you want to go). I think they figure anyone who has gotten high grades in Latin must have a disciplined mind, i.e., a mind that can learn something it doesn't want to know, a talent rated high by the boards of admissions at the best colleges. Girls who have discipline will come out well rounded (like potatoes?). They'll be experts at spending their time and energy on things they care not for. I don't know, you hear a lot about Women's Lib, but I don't see too much of it in Maplewood.

After failing the Latin test I sat on the floor in Gym and watched the girls play volleyball (get that ball over that net!). I didn't play that day because the week before I had fractured my finger and it was still puffed up and sore. After Gym I remember my math teacher (sixty-eight, space shoes and hairnet and a funny bent way of walking) held me up for public ridicule because, not having done my homework in a month, I had no knowledge of an important thing called pi R squared. They never hold you up for public ridicule here at NWS which I consider good. They try to make the classes interesting while attempting to get at the root of your discomfort with yourself. That can be rough but it seems to be helping me, slowly, that and the meditation. Anyway (I get off the track a lot, but then who's judge of what the track is?), this normal stupid day in school had continued with a boring assembly (the chairs are not suitable for sleeping) where we had a lecture by a gray-haired lady in a tweed suit on birds of all nations. She couldn't do birdcalls. After assembly we had lunch (two minuscule, overly firm pizzas, enough to feed one of the birds discussed earlier) and then on to English, study hall and school bus. In English our teacher, Miss Pergament (twenty-three, timid, born and raised in Brooklyn with a lisp) endeavored to extract from us Blake's deeper meaning. Assumably she knew it, but I have my doubts. Study hall was uneventful, school bus was bumpy. Another day of boredom brought toward its end.

"Bev gave me the sweetest party," Jennifer said unexpectedly. "There were thirty girls in all and they each brought a dessert."

"How sweet," said my mother.

"It was," said Jennifer. "They had the cutest little flags on toothpicks and they stuck them right into the food. On each flag was the name of the girl who made the dessert so we knew where to give out compliments. It was adorable. Trisha's muffins didn't rise, but nobody said anything." (Thank God for that.) "There's a sale at the Clothes Tree. I have to go tomorrow. Fall things are going. Bev had the most adorable pants suit, Mother. It was green."

"How sweet."

"It was."

"I'm going to give this to James," I said, picking up my fishcake.

My mother didn't like that.

"I don't recall excusing you," she said.

"I don't either," I said.

"You will sit at the table until dinner is completed."

I hated dinnertime. So much tension, no one really wanting to be with each other. Everyone interested only in their day, no one else's, and I wasn't interested in anything.

"They're cutting back," my father said without notice. He always does that, like he's having this thought dialogue in his own head and he forgets that no one else is in there.

My mother asked him if he was speaking about his dinner and my father said no, they were "cutting back" at the office. They were firing people is what he meant. The recession reaching Teaneck. I wonder if we'll have another depression. Build your life around your money and jump out a window when it goes away. That makes a lot of sense.

"Not you," my mother said. She was smug, but underneath, nervous. "Your position is secure."

"Oh, dear, I guess," my father said. He pushed the remains of his fishcake to one side and stared at his plate. That was when my mother brought up the psychologist.

"The school called today," she said. (The whole school?) "I talked with a Mr. Stubbard, the assistant principal. They recommend that Thelma see a therapist."

My father was engrossed in his fish. He pushed it from one side of his plate to the other. Then he turned it over.

"Did you hear me?" asked my mother.

"It sounds like a good idea to me," said Jennifer.

"Who asked you?" I said.

"I just said it sounds like a good idea. I can have an opinion."

"Mr. Stubbard felt—"

"Stubbins," I said.

"What?" said my mother.

"His name is Stubbins. You might as well get it right."

"There'll be no freshness from you, young lady. That will be that."

I felt like grabbing her by the back of the neck and shoving her face into her creamed spinach. She neatly dabbed the corner of her mouth with her Hudson paper napkin ("linen napkin luxury at a paper napkin price").

"Several teachers were consulted. I learned some mighty unpleasant things, young lady. Each and every teacher said that you do not do your schoolwork and that you are disruptive in class. What do you have to say to that?"

I didn't answer.

"Answer me!"

"Well, now," said my father. I thought he was going to say more, but he didn't.

"I will tell you, young lady," said my mother, "that what you need is willpower. Pure and simple. You don't need any therapists or counselors, or anything else. You are spoiled rotten. I won't have it. Not in my house! You will shape up and shape up fast!"

"It might help her," said Jennifer, sipping her Fresca. "Maybe she can't help herself. When you're that far gone . . ."

"Shut up!" I said.

"Look at her. She's a mess!"

"Now Jennifer," said my father. He hates it when we fight, especially at dinner. It ruins his digestion.

"Well, here is my opinion," said my mother. "You can take it or leave it." (Fat chance.) "The school insists upon testing Thelma. If she doesn't need glasses she may need a therapist." (Aren't there any other possibilities?) "Let them test her if they see fit. They can make their evaluation and we can still do as we like. She's our daughter."

My father was staring at his fishcake and didn't hear.

CHAPTER FOUR

After dinner my mother made me clear the table and wash the dishes. Jennifer was exhausted from her party, poor dear, and had to take a bath. Jennifer is a bath person. She soaks for hours in endless combinations of oils, beads, moisturizers and bubbles. Sometimes when she's in there I think she's fallen asleep and drowned, but no such luck. I feel what's missing so far in what I've "jotted down" (are you there, Dr. Stone?) is a sampling of Jennifer's overt hostility to me. She's a bitch, she really is.

Anyway, after all the clearing and washing and mopping I took my fishcake out to James. I took it along with his dinner, two cans of Alpo (decidedly gross), one cup of Purina Dog Chow and four squirts of heartworm medicine, which I always feed him at that time. He was waiting for me.

"Down, Jimmy, down!" He jumped all over me again and I kneed him in the chest. It doesn't hurt him, but it gives him the idea.

I set down Jimmy's food bowl, but Jimmy didn't eat. He

just stared up at me with this religious look on his face. He knew about the fishcake.

"Here, Jim," I said, and held out the fishcake. He snapped at it and swallowed it in one gulp. I'm glad somebody appreciated it. "Now you can eat, Jim," I said. "No more fish." He got the message and set to work on his humongous food bowl.

I remember sitting down then on the floor of the garage and taking out a book of matches. I had them in my pocket from when we had a smoke out by the football field at lunch. I lit a match and let it burn down as far as possible without burning my fingers. Well, it did burn my fingers a little. I stood it for as long as possible and then let the match drop to the cement floor. Soon it went out. Jimmy didn't pay any attention, of course. He was still eating.

I love fire. I'm sitting in the rec room now and there's a fire going. I write awhile and then stop and stare into the fire. I can sit that way for hours sometimes, like it hypnotizes me. In a way it's like a meditation. It clears everything out. I've always loved fire. It changes things so deeply, so quickly. Fire, the great purifier. That's what the thing was at Ethical Culture, an attempt to purify, but it didn't work out. I guess because my motives weren't pure. If my motives had been free from taint everything would have been all right. It's hard to imagine pure motives for setting fire to a building, especially if it doesn't belong to you, but it's possible. With me there was all this rage mixed in, hatred of Jennifer, hatred of the shallow values and standards she was adopting, fear that I would be sucked in to the same thing, JEALOUSY OF HER BEAUTIFUL AND GORGEOUS LOOKS, JEALOUSY OF MY PARENTS' APPROVAL

OF HER, the desire to attract attention and GET EVEN! These were all strong so everything fell apart.

James finished eating and started licking my face. Now I love him a lot, but I find that gross and disgusting. Alpo Breath!

"No, James! Get Away!"

Jim lay down at my side and I sat there with him for a long time. I noticed his "I Belong To" tag had come off.

"I have to get you a new tag, James." I grabbed him by the ears and kissed him on the side of his nose. "You're my best friend, James, and that's the truth."

I decided to spend the night in the garage and went back into the house to get my sleeping bag. Jennifer was asleep on the living room couch (such a hard day), my father was asleep (in the larger sense, I mean his eyes were open, behind his paper—Dow-Jones Industrial Averages Down One Third) and my mother was studying scraps of fabric. She was RE-DOING THE DEN (and drapes must be coordinated, you bet your life and your boots!).

"Where do you think you're going?" she asked. (Friendly, sweet of tone, gentle in manner.)

"The garage," I muttered. (Charming and gracious.)

"The last time you slept in the garage you woke up with a sore throat. This is October."

I know the month. I may be mean, but I'm not stupid.

"It's warm out," I said. I was lying.

"It's your body," said my mother. "If you want to mistreat it, it's up to you."

I left, slamming the door behind me.

"Don't slam the door!"

Jim knew I was coming back, of course. He shook himself

and jumped on me and moaned. I didn't sleep with him that often. It was a treat for him, I know. I wonder how he is. I miss him so much.

The next morning I woke up with a cold. I knew Mother would be pleased.

"Good news, Mom," I said when I left James to go inside and get my orange juice. "I've got a cold. Doesn't that thrill and delight you? Right once again."

"No smart talk, miss," she said.

"I can't go to school."

"Then you'd better go to bed."

"O.K.!"

I spent the day in bed with my *National Lampoons* and my *Photoplays*, solitaire, chicken bouillon and orange juice. Not a bad time, actually. The last time I was sick I was sent home from school, but I didn't want to go home because my Aunt Minna and Uncle Ed were in from Cleveland and they drive me up the wall. You'll hear more about them soon, but for now I'll just tell you they're my mother's brother and his wife and they are dumber than any two people I have met in this lifetime. Anyway, they were visiting and I didn't want to go home because they get my room when they come and I have no place to get away from them so I went to my friend Janice's.

There's someone else I miss. I didn't mention her before because she moved shortly after this day I'm going to tell you about to Silver Springs, Maryland. She liked photography—she probably still does, but I don't know because I haven't seen her in over six months. Anyway, this other time I was sick I was sent home from school. I had a cold and a sore throat and I didn't want to stay for this stupid history test so

I told the nurse I was throwing up. They hate it when you throw up at school. The nurse sent me home and I went to Janice's to avoid Minna and Ed. Janice was home sick so I knew I'd have company, but I didn't know about THE LUNCHEON. This luncheon was another thing that contributed to my setting fire to Ethical Culture.

When I got to the house the front door was open so I walked in. Janice was sitting under the piano with her pajamas on and through the large glass windows I could see the group of "girls" seated in a circle on the flagstone terrace. It looked like show-and-tell at nursery school.

"Be quiet," said Janice from underneath the piano.

"What are you doing under the piano?"

"Come 'ere."

I crawled in beside her.

"This is unreal," she said, "and I'm out of film."

"What is this?" I asked.

"My mother's giving a luncheon. This is some of the stuff they do when we're in school. You get a good view from under here."

"Won't they see us?"

"Most likely not," she said, "but if they do just smile pleasantly and wave. They don't care what we do."

We spent over two hours under that piano. The luncheon lasted from twelve-thirty to six, but I really felt sick and I had to leave after two hours. O.K. This is what we saw.

At one end of the circle were Sarah Smith, Terry Vincent, Evelyn Trancus and Rosalie Cushman. They were all stylishly dressed in pants suits, or matching sports ensembles of some kind. The faces were different, but the clothes were the same.

"Andrew had a month off, but we stayed in Maplewood," Rosalie Cushman was saying.

"You didn't go anywhere?"

The girls were stunned.

"No."

"Not all summer?"

"No."

"Not even for a weekend?"

"I wanted to, but I didn't want to say anything."

"You stayed in the house with your husband for a month?" Sarah was horrified.

"I sunbathed. That's what I do mostly. I can sunbathe right through November. We have a niche. Andrew doesn't like the way I look without a tan."

"I think you look cute."

"You've never seen me without a tan."

"That's true."

"I look awful."

"I wouldn't know what to do for all that time at home with my husband," said Sarah. "We never stay home for more than a weekend. We always go somewhere."

"Where do you go?"

"The beach, or someplace, but it's always so damp."

"That's true."

"I hate the dampness, but it's good for the kids."

"Not the dampness."

"No, not the dampness. The ocean. They love it."

"I'd like to go to the Galápagos Islands to see the Komodo dragons," said Evelyn (I swear to God!), "but I haven't been out of New Jersey in ten years. Maybe when the kids grow up."

I wanted to tell her that the kids would probably love to see the Komodo dragons, no need to wait on their account, but I figured it wasn't worth getting out from under the piano and causing a commotion and it wouldn't make any difference anyway.

I guess my favorite part of the luncheon was the great zucchini debate. To begin with, Janice's mother, Clover, had put her plastic serving trays in the dishwasher and they had come out all warped and funny, free-form, hideous sculptures. WHAT SHOULD SHE DO NOW? She had intended them for the hors d'oeuvres, zucchini and plum tomatoes, but would the trays be suitable in their present condition, never mind that, would they even do the job? Would the plum tomatoes simply roll off? It was finally decided, with the help of Nancy Lovebin (I like that name and swear before God I didn't make it up), that since nothing else in the house was suitable as an hors d'oeuvres tray they should throw caution to the wind, what the hell, and use the plastic trays anyway.

"What's the worst that could happen?" asked Nancy.

"The tomatoes could roll off," said Rosalie.

"Right," said Nancy. "Big deal. So we have tomatoes on the floor. The girls would laugh. They're a swell bunch."

"You be in charge then," said Sarah. "I don't want it on my head."

But THE VERY TERRIBLE THING was that Nancy didn't know how you were SUPPOSED to cut the zucchini. WAS IT THE LONG WAY OR IN DISCS? I love that, really. I mean, how can there be a way you're supposed to cut zucchini? I can see a board of judges with glasses and pads of paper, The Great Zucchini Panel, who formulate instructions on all dealings with zucchini and pass them down. In desperation Nancy put the question to Terry Vincent, "who knows about zucchini," although she has two emotionally disturbed, retarded and vicious children. I mean people spend their time this way!

CHAPTER FIVE

Right before Jennifer's wedding I stayed at home with my cold for three days and then Mother sent me back to school. I remember still having a cough and swollen sinuses and riding home on the school bus with the kids screaming and passing this sign by the side of the road that said "MEN WORKING IN TREES." Why must we know the sex of the people in the trees? Do they have "WOMEN WORKING IN TREES" signs? It's doubtful since women, as a rule, don't work in trees. I'd like working in a tree.

When I got home Jennifer was in the living room with Kevin. Kevin is about twenty-four years old with very short brown hair and glasses. He almost looks Jewish (I don't really know what I mean, it's just you look at him and you think "he's Jewish") but he isn't, a fact which Jennifer makes a whole big deal about. He dresses very neatly, but in bad taste—thin belts, shiny socks, slacks, no jeans. What he looks like, mostly, is a turtle. He has that startled carefulness of your average turtle and he hovers beneath his protective shell. I told him once that he strongly resembled a turtle, but he didn't appreciate it. He doesn't like me, that's for sure. He was around the house a lot then, mostly on weekends. He would spend Saturday afternoon just sitting around, or helping my father with the hedge trimming. We had these hedges, some of the only green stuff on Pinetree Road, and my father used to go out on Saturday afternoons and trim them. He used these automatic hedge trimmers, and he's too vague to work on any kind of mechanical thing, so Kevin would always end up doing it with my father standing around staring out into the middle distance. James HATED the noise of those trimmers. He would stand in the yard and bark at Kevin the whole time Kevin did the trimming. One Saturday James barked for over three hours straight. I was going to town to buy some gum and magazines and when I left the house Kevin was at the front hedge and James was about two feet away staring at him and barking like crazy.

"Why don't you get some earmuffs?" I shouted.

"What?" said Kevin.

"Why don't you get some earmuffs?"

"I can't hear you."

"Why don't you get some earmuffs?"

Kevin turned off the trimmers. Jimmy stopped barking and came over and leaned on me. He does that a lot. He backs into people and leans on them. I think it's an old sheep herding instinct.

"That's some dog you've got there," said Kevin. He never did like James.

"The noise getting to you?"

"I'll say," said Kevin. He scrunched his face up and took off his John Deere cap and wiped the sweat off his forehead with the sleeve of his shirt.

"You should get some earmuffs. That's what I was trying to tell you."

"Earmuffs?"

"Sure. Bring them along for the next trim."

"It's August."

"They'll cut the noise."

"Now, really, I'd look pretty silly here, wouldn't I? Trimming the hedge in August, wearing earmuffs."

"It's not a fashion show."

"Very funny," said Kevin. He turned the trimmers back on and James started barking again and I went off to get my magazines and gum.

Well, this day I started to tell you about when I came home from school and Kevin and Jennifer were in the living room it was three weeks before THE WEDDING. Jennifer and my mother had originally wanted a church wedding, but a cousin of Kevin's had had this "real nice ceremony" at Ethical Culture and recommended it so highly to Kevin that Kevin insisted they have THE WEDDING there. Jennifer, being the pushover that she is, of course agreed. When I came home that afternoon Kevin and Jennifer were going over a pamphlet from the Holiday Inn (where the reception was going to be) called *Just To Make Sure You Remember Everything Here's a Checklist For Your Wedding Day.* I remember looking at the pamphlet later that same night. It looked like this. It may not be exactly right, but this is close:

JUST TO MAKE SURE YOU REMEMBER EVERYTHING, HERE'S A CHECKLIST FOR YOUR WEDDING DAY!

Bride's Checklist

Announce engagement in local paper
Select date and make reservation for church or wherever ceremony is to be held
Select and order invitations and thank you stationery
Select your gown and those of your bridesmaids (What about sisters?)
Discuss music with organist and soloist
Visit or telephone your newspaper and provide vital information
Start shopping for your trousseau
Assist both mothers in their dress selections (What about sisters?)
Make arrangements for your wedding cake
Address the wedding invitations (What about mailing them?)
Check on arrangements for rehearsal

Groom's Checklist

Purchase engagement ring
Get marriage license
Purchase wedding ring
Purchase wedding apparel for yourself
Make honeymoon reservations with Holiday Inn

There might be more things for the bride, I'm not sure, and maybe even less for the groom. It's funny why she gets all the work.

I went into the kitchen to look for some chocolate cake, but there wasn't any. I blew my poor nose on a napkin, got a cookie and one for James and started back through the living room, coughing and feeling miserable. Jennifer and Kevin were talking about whether or not they wanted music and what kind.

"I'd like show tunes," said Jennifer. "A small band would be nice and maybe Marge could sing."

"Your friend, Marge?"

"You know Marge."

"She sounds like a frog."

"She has a lovely voice."

"You can't be serious. Why her husband wasted his money on voice lessons for her I'll never know."

"It's her money too."

"He earned it."

I backed into the kitchen to eavesdrop in safety. This was a juicy conversation. The self-centered pig was showing his true colors.

"It upsets me when you talk like that," said Jennifer.

"Don't be silly."

"She likes to sing."

"Let's drop it. You're in no mood to discuss this."

"What if I want to take some kind of lessons? Are you going to say I can't because I'm no good at it?"

"Grow up, will you?"

"Why would I need lessons if I could already do something?"

"Like what? What are you talking about?"

"I don't know. Anything."

"Like what?"

"Painting. Let's say I wanted to take painting lessons."

"You'll have enough to do without messing around with paint. Don't be childish."

Their life together flashed before my eyes. No communication, no respect, no caring. They didn't love each other. You need those things for love. I'd rather be dead than trapped in a marriage like that. I headed for the garage. Kevin noticed me and called out a polite "hello."

"Hello," I said. I didn't stop walking.

"Did you have a nice time at school?"

Kevin hates me. He did then and still does, still considers me with loathing from his rumpus room in Tenafly. I consider him with loathing too so I guess that's fair. Well, not so much now. I don't loathe anything or anyone with the same old verve of yesteryear. I can't say I like him, though. He looks down on women, children and animals; he's dishonest, stupid, prejudiced, selfish, closed-minded and worst of all, closed-hearted. Larry, my teacher up here (more of him later!) says that's the worst of it, a closed heart. I understand that now, but I'm getting ahead of myself.

Anyway, my day at school had been particularly rotten. In addition to feeling lousy two really disgusting things happened. First (and foremost), I had three hours of "comprehensive tests" by a stout woman named Consuela Bevermanns and, second, I got up to go to the bathroom (that's not the disgusting part) and punctured my finger with my lead pencil. It was gross. Consuela Bevermanns got all upset and sent me down to the nurse.

"I stuck a pencil in my finger," I announced to the nurse. She was sitting at a desk near the window in her white uniform and tiny nurse's cap.

"Whadja do that for?" she said. She got up and walked over to me without ever standing up straight. Arthritic deposits? "Had a tetanus shot lately?" she asked. She grabbed my hand and began twisting it roughly. "Which finger is it?"

"This one."

"Let me see." She pulled my finger up near her nose. I think her eyesight was poor.

"Yes."

"What?"

"I had a tetanus shot this summer. I stepped on a nail."

"All right. Wash your hands and go back to class. Where's your slip?"

"I don't have one. I was having a test."

"You're supposed to get a slip."

"I don't have one."

"Forget it. Wash your hands."

I washed my hands and went back to Consuela, who was drinking a cup of coffee to calm herself down. She drank a lot of coffee and she smoked a lot too.

At that point I had things floating around in two out of my ten fingers, a piece of bone in one from when I fractured it in volleyball and a piece of carbon in the other. It may actually have only been dust from the tip of my pencil (it was freshly sharpened), but that would be carbon dust and that's carbon. So there we are.

I ignored Kevin's question about the roughness of my day and started out to visit with James.

"What are you wearing to the wedding by the way?" said Jennifer.

"Nothing much," I said, and let the door slam behind me.

James wagged his tail from where he sat, staring up at me, drooling, with his religious cookie-expectation expression all over his face.

James, I love you.

I gave him his cookie and sat down on the front steps to eat mine. I heard my mother through the window on the upstairs phone, talking with the drapery man. She had both the wheat and the tan samples, but decisions weren't easy.

Jennifer opened the front door and stuck her head out.

"What do you mean by that?" she demanded.

I paid no attention—the great debate was about to begin.

"Would you come in here a minute, please?" said Jennifer.

When I got inside this whole big thing started with Jennifer insisting on knowing what I was going to wear to her wedding and me insisting that it was none of her business.

"If you plan to come to my wedding looking like a slob you've got another think coming," Jennifer announced.

I turned and headed for the kitchen.

"Where do you think you're going?"

"To get a cookie," I said.

"Come here and let's finish this."

I just went right on into the kitchen. I took five cookies out of the bread box and Jennifer appeared.

"What are you wearing?"

"Jeans and a T-shirt."

"Not now, stupid, I mean to the wedding."

"Jeans and a T-shirt."

"You are not."

"All right, then I won't come. I don't have to be there."

"You most certainly do have to be there! What do you mean, you don't have to be there?"

"I don't have to be there."

"You're my sister! Of course you have to be there!"

"I don't see how that follows."

"You are dense."

"Why does it follow that because I'm your sister I have to be at your wedding? We don't get along. I don't owe you any money. Why should I be there?"

That was when Jennifer turned and stormed out of the kitchen. I could hear her crying through the swinging door. Then Kevin started comforting her, or trying to.

"There, there, what is it now?"

"Thelma says she's wearing jeans to the wedding or she's not coming and she means it."

"Now, Jennifer." (He always said that, not plain "Jennifer" but always "Now Jennifer" like that was her name.) "Now, Jennifer, I'm sure she's only teasing. She'll come and look most attractive, I'm sure."

"I haven't seen her in a dress in two years." (It was longer than that.)

"Do you want me to talk to her?"

"Yes."

"All right. I'll talk to her."

After that Kevin came into the kitchen in his gabardine slacks and pullover. You couldn't see his narrow belt, but undoubtedly he had one on underneath the pullover. Why do I hate narrow belts? Anyway, he came into the kitchen and for some totally bizarre reason sat himself up on top of the dishwasher. I think it might have been a "don't-worry-about-me-I'm-just-one-of-the-gang" sort of gesture. Anyway, I'd never seen him do anything like that before.

"Rough day at school, huh?"

(Jennifer was still crying in the living room.)

"Yeah," I said. I had finished my cookies and was sitting at the kitchen table, eating a banana.

"School can be rough. People don't realize it. They forget,

but school can be rough. I remember."

"You're still in school."

"You're right. You're a smart cookie."

I wanted to tell him I wasn't a cookie, but I figured what the hell. Mostly I just wanted him to go away.

"Well," he said, "Jennifer's a little upset in there."

"I can hear that."

"That's right. Well she's a little upset in there. Some silliness about what you're going to wear to the wedding. Now I couldn't care less" (a lie) "but Jennifer seems to think you'll only wear jeans."

"I'll wear a shirt too."

"No, I know you'll wear a shirt. That's not what I mean. I mean I said she said you said you'd only wear jeans, but of course I meant with a shirt or something."

"Or a sweater."

"Or a sweater."

"Or a T-shirt."

"Or a T-shirt."

"Or a sweat shirt."

"Or a sweat shirt, or what have you."

"Or what have you."

"Right. Now I know you were kidding, but she doesn't. She's awful upset in there and you could help her feel a heck of a lot better if you'd just apologize. Tell her you were kidding."

I just kept eating my banana. I didn't know what to say. Of course I hadn't been kidding, but I figured if I just told Kevin that all of a sudden with him sitting up there on the dishwasher and all, he might get all upset and fall off the dishwasher—total retard that he is—so I just kept chewing on my banana and looking out the window at Scott Smith beating up Penny's younger brother, Ronald. Ronald is a sweet little kid. He's about four years old. Scott is always beating up on defenseless youngsters. I kept staring at them and eating my banana and coughing now and then because of my disgusting cold, and then Kevin said something like, "What do you say?"

"I don't know," I said. "You see, you and Jennifer are having this wedding, but in all honesty I don't want to go. I don't mean to hurt your feelings, it's just that my view of marriage is rotten. I mean I've been watching my mother and father all these years and from what I've seen it doesn't work out. That's the first thing, and the second thing is that I would hate the reception. There'll be lots of people standing around and drinking and laughing and talking at each other and saying what a nice couple you and Jennifer make. I wouldn't have a good time. See Jennifer says I have to come because I'm her sister, but I don't see how that follows. I have to come and I have to wear a certain costume. I don't like that. If I liked Jennifer" (or you for the matter, but I didn't say that), "if I liked her or if she was a friend of mine, then I should go just to make her happy, but we don't like each other. I don't see the sense of going to this thing just because I'm her sister if I don't see the sense of it."

Kevin didn't like any of that. There was this long pause with him up there on the dishwasher and then he said, "We'll work it out, no problem," and got down off the dishwasher and went into the living room to see "Now Jennifer."

So there I was sitting in the kitchen with my cough and my running nose and no chocolate cake and nothing to do except watch the neighborhood bully beat up on poor defenseless children. I heard Jennifer crying in the living room and Kevin telling her it would work out, and then I heard my mother come in from the den.

"Thelma's being a bitch," Jennifer said through her tears.

"Jennifer, please!" said Mother.

"Well, she is. She says she'll wear jeans to the wedding or she won't come."

"She damn well will come," (language, Mother) "and in suitable attire. I'll see to that."

"You hear that?" said Kevin. "Now, Jennifer, calm down."

Jennifer blew her nose.

"You will not believe my afternoon," said Mother.

"What happened?" asked Kevin.

"I went to the Paramus Mall for Christmas cards and it was one thing after the next."

"What happened?"

"It was crowded for one thing. You wouldn't believe the crowds."

"Oh, dear."

"Indeed. Well, I could not find the card counter, so after looking everywhere I asked the information girl."

"Good idea."

"She sent me to the wrong floor."

"No!"

"Can you imagine?"

Kevin chuckled a few times and clicked his tongue. He is such a prune.

"I looked by myself."

"No."

"What was I to do?"

"Oh, my."

"But wait." Mother began to laugh. "Isn't this something?"

"It certainly is."

"I finally found the counter."

"Thank goodness."

"Yes."

"Boy oh boy."

"I finally found the counter and spent one hour selecting our card."

"Oh, no."

"Yes, but when I found it they were out of it!"

"No!"

"Can you imagine? In October!"

My father came home that night with news that he might be fired the following week. He was sort of upset, but then he's always sort of upset so it's hard to tell. My mother was upset too, but remained firm in her conviction that it was all a tempest in a teapot. Kevin stayed for dinner, frozen turkey pies, and then he and Jennifer went to the movies. My mother and father went over to the Cushmans' for coffee (coffee, coffee everywhere) and I was left to my own vices.

I was feeling pretty rotten with my cold and was under strict orders to do my homework and go straight to bed. I called up Jonathan to see what he was doing. A friend of his, a humongous football player named Robert, was over at his house. Jonathan said they would ride their bikes over and say hi. I knew they wouldn't stay long though. Jonathan and I were spending less and less time together. He had a couple of GORGEOUS GIRL FRIENDS (neither of which was me) and had given up football. I used to love to play football with Jonathan and about four or five other guys on his street, but around this time they had started not wanting to play with me anymore. They were playing football at high school, or they weren't playing football at all, being into tennis mostly, or if they were playing football they didn't want to play with me because of my being a girl. It's weird. I really missed Janice, although I didn't admit it to myself much. We used to hang around a lot and wonder what to do, but she was company. Up here at NWS I'm starting to have real friends and there's things we like to do together, besides sex, that is. Of course sex is the really BIG THING with kids my age. It's like mostly what their minds are on—mine too, I suppose. (I like the way I left myself out of the whole business. Hello, Dr. Stone.) It's weird. I can't picture Jennifer and Kevin doing it. They must, but I can't picture them and I simply cannot picture my parents or any of the "girls" on the block, except maybe Nancy Lovebin. Me and Jonathan have done it a couple of times and it's O.K., but the BIG DEAL escapes me. Maybe we don't love each other (that's for sure) or maybe I just haven't had an orgasm yet. Maybe then I'll understand. That may be IT. My problems and questions answered, but I doubt it. I was drawn into it a lot in Maplewood with Jonathan, and Walter Sand and Jeremy Kite sometimes, but we never went "all the way." I don't know. It can sure take over, wondering how it will be, remembering how it was, picturing different people and all. Everyone's a lot more open about it up here at NWS. I haven't slept with anybody up here and I don't really want to at this point, but tomorrow I may feel differently. I'd like it to be wonderful.

Be that as it may, I hung up the phone and waited for Jonathan Bessmer and his humongous football player friend, Robert, to darken my doorstep.

CHAPTER SIX

For lack of anything better to do I turned on the T.V. Cher was on with all her hair and her outfits and everything. I cannot fathom her popularity. Most of T.V. is crap, however I used to watch it a great deal. We don't have T.V. up here at NWS, which is a good thing. Back "home" I would watch knowing the shows stank. I like the cockatoo on "Baretta." He's nice. I also like "Candid Camera" and some of the game shows where the fat ladies jump up and down and scream and have conniption fits when they win those wonderful objects.

There I was watching Cher and starting to get hungry, so I went into the kitchen and had some cereal and milk and then took four cookies, a root beer, some pretzels and a pickle and went back to watch T.V. I could hear Jimmy outside in the garage barking messages to some dog on Commodore Lane.

The bell rang and it was the guys. They were hot and sweaty.

"How's it going?" asked Jonathan.

"The usual crap," I said.

"Got anything to drink? I could use a brew."

We went into the kitchen and there wasn't any beer, so I gave them Cokes and got out the cookies and we sat down and chewed the fat (and the cookies). Robert kept drumming rhythms on the table all the while. It was hard to hear anything else. Jonathan was hysterical over the weekend he had spent with his father (he lives with his mother and stepfather) and his father's girl friend.

"You won't believe this weekend," he said, his mouth full of cookies.

"What happened?"

"We went to the Bahamas."

"For the weekend?"

"We flew and Susan, my father's girl friend, spent the whole weekend taking baths and having her hair done."

"She sounds like Jennifer."

"I swear to God. The entire weekend. That's all she did. I don't even think she ate."

"Maybe she was on a diet."

"Probably. She looks the type. Skinny. I mean, why did she go, you know what I mean? She didn't spend any time with my father. She didn't look at the Bahamas or swim or anything. Why didn't she stay in Newark?"

"Beats me."

"She is so dumb. Dad and I had a nice time, though. When you think about it, I guess it worked out pretty well. He never would have taken me alone."

"How about some popcorn," I suggested.

"Sounds good," said Robert. He was still drumming.

There were two of those Jiffy Pop things in the aluminum foil pans with the blue-and-white cardboard tops in the cupboard, so we heated them up. One of them exploded all over the kitchen, but the other one turned out pretty good.

The doorbell rang and I answered it and there was Jennifer all pale and green and Kevin gripping her by the elbow.

"What's the matter?" I said. "I thought you went to the movies."

"Jennifer fainted," said Kevin. "Help me get her on the couch."

I closed the door and grabbed Jennifer by the other elbow and we helped her to the couch. Jennifer used to faint a lot before she went to college. Well, not a lot, really, but it seemed that way. She fainted twice, once at Radio City Music Hall and once at midterms. She used to have a lot of spells though where she thought she was going to faint. She'd get dizzy and everything. They had her checked out, but the doctor said she was fine. (A lot he knew.) She used to throw up a lot too. She took these ballet classes in Newark and she used to throw up very often before class. This time I started to tell you about marked her third faint unless she had fainted at college without my knowing which is entirely possible.

Kevin was really upset. He guided Jennifer to the couch. "We need some water here right away!"

I brought in the water and sat down on the couch next to Jennifer.

"Did she faint at the movies?" I asked, but Kevin ignored me.

"Now, Jennifer, have some of this water." "Now Jennifer" took the water and began to drink. She looked very pale.

"Are you O.K.?" I asked.
"She'll be fine," said Kevin.
Jonathan and Robert came into the living room and stood, hovering around with their Cokes and popcorn.
"What happened?" asked Jonathan.
"She fainted," said Kevin.
"Where did she faint?" I asked. "At the movies?"
"She was in the ladies room," said Kevin. "That's where she fainted."
"Where were you?"
"I was in the theater."
"You weren't in the ladies room."
"Of course not."
"If you weren't in the ladies room how did you know she fainted? Did someone tell you? Were you peeking through the door?"
"I wasn't peeking through any door."
"Someone told you."
"Yes. I went up to the door and a lady came out and I asked if she'd seen Jennifer."
"And she had."
"Yes. She said Jennifer had fainted, but she was about to come out. So she came out and we came home and here we are. I think it would help if you'd leave us alone." He was getting testy.
"Suit yourself," I said. "Do you need anything, Jennifer?"
"No," said Jennifer.
"Now, Jennifer, just stretch out here on the couch."
Jennifer stretched out there on the couch and my parents came in.
"I'll be getting on home now," said Jonathan.

"Me too," said Robert. "I have to get up early and mow the lawn." (A likely story.)

"What are you doing up, young lady?" said my mother. She handed my father her coat without looking at him. I hate it when she does that, like he's her footman, or something, hanging around, waiting for coats. "It is one hour past your bedtime. How dare you have company at this hour?"

"We're just leaving, Mrs. Beldwin," said Jonathan. "Sorry to trouble you."

"Good night, Mrs. Beldwin," said Robert, and they were gone.

My mother looked at me with fury and loathing.

"Go to bed, this minute," she said.

"Jennifer fainted," I said. "I would have been asleep hours ago, but I had to take care of her."

That did it. One mention of Jennifer and my mother forgot all about me.

"Stay right there, Jennifer. I'll get you some brandy," she said, and she went out to the kitchen.

My father was standing near the front door, still holding my mother's coat. His mind was somewhere else, probably on losing his job, but who knows.

"Jennifer fainted," I said, louder this time.

"Oh, my," said my father. He sat down in the nearest chair, still holding the coat. "Can I get you something?"

"She'll be fine," said Kevin.

"Oh, dear," said my father, and my mother came back in with the brandy. She poured it for Jennifer and held it while she drank it and all the while went into this whole thing about the wedding and how I was going and how I was not going to wear jeans. Her sense of priorities is weird. Here

Jennifer is trying to tell her something, the least of which is "Help me I'm so tense I keep fainting, my nerves are all mixed up, I don't know if I'm doing what I want with my life today or any other day, I want to escape." All my mother can think about is my wardrobe.

I looked over what I've written so far last night and I felt a really weird thing. My parents are like strangers. I think about them less being up here. That's a very good thing about living away from "home." There's not always these strangers around who I'm supposed to know, and feel close to, long to feel close to, beneath all the rest of it. I long for an open line of understanding, of mutual respect, just to be thought of as a human person. I'm so jealous of kids who have that. I try to remember the good times. There were some. I remember one New Year's Eve my parents gave a New Year's Eve party.

My father was the bartender and I was his assistant. The afternoon before the party we made up a whole menu which he let me type on his typewriter and we got to laughing about all the things that people could want.

"Ovaltine," my father said, suddenly.

"What?"

"Ovaltine. Someone might want it. Who's to say they won't? Can we say that?" (I suspect a sense of humor lurks beneath his wall of vagaries.)

"Not really."

"We can't."

"Not for sure."

"Put it down."

O-V-A-L-T-I-N-E, I typed.

Later at the party it was my job to take the menu around

to everybody and then get the orders from my father and bring them to the people. I felt like I had a really important job and that made it fun and everyone would read the menu and laugh when they saw the Ovaltine.

"What's this?" they would ask. "Ovaltine? That's funny."

"You want some?"

"Ha. Ha. What a clever menu. I'll have a scotch and soda."

Back to the bar I would go with my orders, a symphony of chuckling in the background.

"Ovaltine! That's cute!"

"How many Ovaltines?" my father would ask, and double up with laughter.

"Not too many," I'd say.

My father would go on laughing, and then I'd start in because he was so funny when he laughed. There we'd be, laughing and spilling drinks all over the place. It was great.

That was the only time I remember him laughing except when we played Crazy Eights. My father loved that game. He still may for that matter. I make it sound like he's dead. (Hi, Dr. Stone.) I don't know why, but every time we played (Crazy Eights is a card game, is that common knowledge?), we would get to giggling and laughing and we almost couldn't stop. I don't know why. I mean it's not in itself a funny game. I remember during one game we got to talking about the dog next door. My father had just dealt the cards and was examining his hand.

"Have you seen Phyllis lately?" he asked, and began to laugh.

"She got a haircut," I said. I was grouping my cards by pairs.

"I stepped out yesterday and there she was by the mailbox. She startled me. Why did they give her that trim? She looks like a peach."

"That's true."

By now my father had set down his cards. He was laughing his head off (as they say).

"She looks like a peach with this puffed thing on the end of her tail."

"I know." By now I was laughing too.

"It's the darnedest thing."

"She looks more like Mrs. Trautman this way," I said. Mrs. Trautman is Phyllis' owner.

"Darned if she doesn't," said my father.

We must have laughed for ten minutes. No wonder I love that game. Crazy Eights is still my favorite.

When I was little my father used to take me on outings like to the park or Newark Airport.

"Are those planes held up on coat hangers?" I would ask. (I was three or something.)

"No. Pilots drive them. Men with caps. They fly like birds."

Since I was eleven or so we never spend much time together. Before I left for up here the only other good times would be eating chocolate cake together as a nighttime snack. We didn't speak to each other, but we were at the same table, enjoying our cake. Maybe my father was good looking once. Now he's forty-five and sort of soft looking, like putty. Not fat, but weak, soft as I said, his true personality coloring his looks. His main charm is his childlike quality. He needs looking after and I don't know how to do that.

My mother does. I guess you have to give her credit. Now,

have we had any good times? NOT RECENTLY! That's for sure!

I can remember playing Monopoly with my mother when I had the measles. She was usually pretty good with a sick person. When I had the measles she was actually enjoyable. She'd bring in the soup, or whatever, and I'd set up the board.

"Do you have Marvin Gardens?" she'd ask.

"Not me."

"It's always the last to go. Why is that? Blow on your soup, it's hot."

Other nice times? She took me to buy ice skates when I was twelve and afterward we went to have ice cream sundaes.

"Let's stop for a sundae," she said. "Buying skates is a special occasion."

"Sure!" (Once a chocolate fan, always a chocolate fan.) "I'm having nuts *and* whipped cream."

Otherwise, I have pretty much negative things to say about my mother. My mother is attractive. She's stylish and all, and very efficient. I'm getting bored with this. (Hi, Dr. Stone. You asked me to JOT down parent stuff, so here it is. I'm getting bored instead of furious. Is that a good sign?) What do they like to do? Not much. My father likes to read the paper and take naps. Sometimes he listens to the radio (music with strings, taste a bit like Jennifer's). He enjoys his orange juice and watching golf matches on T.V. He doesn't play anymore because he has a bad back. He might like his work. He doesn't let on. WHO IS HE?

My mother, as I mentioned earlier, likes bossing other people around and things like REDOING THE DEN, ordering wedding invitations and Christmas cards, writing thank you notes, keeping tabs on relatives and buying clothes for her-self (although she would never admit it).

I'm afraid I don't know who the hell my parents are.

It's time to plunge in and tell about the last two weeks before the wedding. They lead to my flip-out, but then so did the whole rest of my life.

Things were pretty dull. Jennifer fainted two more times and Kevin broke out in a rash. It was all over his neck—no-where else as far as he would admit—just his neck—all red and flaky. It was gross. He was around quite a bit with his rash and Jennifer was fainting and buying things to wear on her honeymoon in the Virgin Islands (appropriate name for a honeymoon spot), and taking baths and making lists and going to luncheons. My father's job was still in jeopardy, Mother was REDOING THE DEN and taking care of last-minute wedding plans and all her regular household duties. I was going crazy.

There were more tests at school. My intellect, my emotions, my nerves, all these were in question. I had tests every other day, most of them administered by my friend, Consuela Bever-manns (how can a human person drink so much coffee?). I could picture Consuela saving up for European summer tours with her Eurailpass, her phrase book of all nations, her heavy walking shoes, raincoat (single row of buttons, not classic trench), leather purse and a camera around her neck. A good scout, Consuela. She also smokes too much.

Everything was wrong with me—you name it. I had a physical too. I didn't have a brain tumor. I used to think I had a brain tumor because I had terrible headaches, those two weeks before the wedding. I was feeling dizzy too. I'd be in school and the whole room would start to spin. I was also having trouble sleeping. I'd lie down and my heart would start to pound and scare me and keep me awake. It was the beginning of November and I hadn't done a night's homework since school began. The teachers were going crazy. Nothing they did could make me do ANYTHING. They would try to be understanding, helpful, angry, threatening and mean, but nothing worked. Every time we'd have a test I'd hand in a blank paper. I hated the work so much! There are no words!

In the midst of this The Great Jeans-Wedding Debate was in full flower. Jennifer told me that if, one, I didn't come to the wedding, or two, I did come to the wedding, but wore jeans, she would kill me. My mother offered to take me shopping but I refused. What I really had in mind was staying home. I planned on getting a violent sickness, more violent than my brain tumor and heart attacks. I even planned to stick my finger down my throat and make myself vomit if the need arose. I knew a few girls in junior high who used to do that. They were on hunger strikes and if their mothers forced them to eat, afterwards they would make themselves throw up. I find that gross, however I understand their point of view. I knew another girl who went on a hunger strike. She would eat only nuts and she kept losing all this weight and her mother had a conniption fit and had to go to a psychiatrist. The girl's father was a psychiatrist, but the mother didn't go to him, she went to a different one. I also knew a girl who killed herself.

CHAPTER SEVEN

A week before the wedding it was time for THE ARRIVAL OF MINNA AND ED. I mentioned they live in Cleveland and are unbelievably dumb and always get my bedroom. Add to this the fact that I was losing my mind and you've got the picture. Minna and Ed were the straws that broke the camel's back, or two of the straws, anyway.

They came into Newark on a Friday night and my parents went to pick them up. Jennifer was out with Kevin. After my parents left for the airport I went out to feed James. I gave him his Alpo and watched him slurp it down. He snapped at it with his front teeth and then threw it back down his throat with a jerk of his head. He doesn't do much chewing. When he was done we went out on the lawn. We played this game where I blow in his face and he snaps at my nose. He pretends to hate it, but he really loves it.

I was feeling pretty tired and I had a bad headache, so we played for a while and then I went in and took a little nap.

I woke up with the same disgusting headache, so I took some aspirins and went into my room. I decided to light some incense. Penny had given it to me—remember the girl I mentioned who was equally happy vacuuming or going to a movie? She burned it in her room a lot, although her younger sister, Heather, said it made her nose itch. I remembered that I was supposed to clean my room because of Minna and Ed taking it over. The thought of spending the next week in the midst of everyone on the living room couch filled me with dread. I began pacing around my room, kicking junk that was on the floor. Fury started welling up in me and I punched my fist into the wall. I thought for a moment that I had broken my knuckles, but they were O.K. I sat down in the midst of all my junk on the floor. I had to relax. Maybe I could meditate. Penny gave me this book to read, *Siddhartha* by Hermann Hesse, and also a book called *Autobiography of a Yogi. Siddhartha* I kind of liked. It was short (a thing I favored in books at the time) and I remember feeling that it had a lot to say. I've forgotten what, but I suspect that's a reflection on my state of mind (or heart) and not on *Siddhartha.* (I must reread that in light of current experiences!) *Autobiography of a Yogi* is the longest book I've ever seen. I read two pages and that was that. Janice said it was her favorite book, better than science fiction. In another few years maybe I'll try it again.

Anyway, I had meditated two times with Janice, but nothing much happened. The first time it was quiet and kind of peaceful and a little floaty, like turning on, which I've also done a couple of times. The second time was awful. Every part of my body itched and I felt like screaming and I had to stop. I was hoping this would be like the first time, floaty, but all that happened was I started to cry, so I got up and went into the living room and stood on my head on the couch. It wasn't a complete headstand. It was this thing I used to do. It made my headaches feel a little better. I do it sometimes now even. It relaxes me. I get on all fours on a bed or a couch, or anything soft, and put my head down between my arms with the top of my head on the soft surface. I just stay that way and let the blood rush to my head.

I was in my head-standing position, rocking back and forth on the living room couch, when Minna and Ed came in.

"There's Thelma," said Minna, pointing to me.

"What's she doing?" asked Ed.

Nobody answered him.

"Thelma, get up," said my mother. "Minna and Ed are here."

I knew Minna and Ed were there, but it was weird. I just couldn't seem to move.

"What's she doing?" repeated Ed. Still nobody answered him.

My father started to set down the suitcases, but my mother said, "Take the bags into Thelma's room. Minna and Ed are sleeping there. Thelma, get up. I hope you cleaned your room."

"What's she doing?" repeated Ed.

"We don't know," said Minna. "Now, hush, Ed. Thelma, how are you, dear? Come over and give your Aunt Minna a big hug."

I got up and went over to Minna.

"Hello, Aunt Minna," I said, and we hugged. I was feeling dizzy from being upside down all that time.

"You've gotten so big." Minna always said that. "We brought you a little gift, but maybe you're too big."

"What's that smell?" asked Ed. He was referring to my incense.

"Hush, Ed," said Minna. "Come over here and say hello to your little niece although she's not so little anymore."

Ed came over and shook my hand.

"Hi, there, Thelma," he said. He still had his hat on. "What's that smell?"

"It's Thelma's," said my mother. "It's something she burns. It's awful. Thelma, put that out. You knew Minna and Ed would be in there tonight. How could you light that?"

"What does she burn?" asked Ed.

Just then my father came out of my room and sat down.

"Well now," he said.

"How's the room, Bill?" asked my mother. "Is it clean?"

"I don't remember," said my father. "Why doesn't everybody sit down?"

"What does she burn?"

"Hush, Ed."

"Why don't we all sit down?"

Ed sat down and then Minna asked him to go into my room and get her suitcase with the "you know what for Thelma in it."

"Go where?" asked Ed. He still had his hat on.

"Go on in Thelma's room and get my suitcase and bring it on in here. It's got the 'you know what for Thelma in it.' "

"What's it got?"

"Hush, now, Ed. I want it to be a surprise. You know. Just go on in there and get it."

"Minna wants her bag, Bill," said my mother. "Go on in and get it."

"Don't trouble yourself," said Ed, and he went in to get

the bag. Minna sat down on the couch and pulled me down next to her and took my hands in hers and said, "Now let me look at you."

(It's a free country.)

"Did you clean your room?" asked my mother. She sat down too.

"No," I said.

"I asked you to clean your room! Now go and do it immediately!"

"Oh, let's give her the gift first. I want to see if they fit."

"What's that stuff you're burning in there?" asked Ed, coming in with Minna's humongous suitcase.

"Put it out and spray some air freshener in there, Thelma," said my mother. "That stuff is awful."

"Oh, let her see her present first," said Minna. She opened her suitcase and started fishing around.

"What's that stuff you're burning in there?" said Ed. He always sounded like a broken record. He never knew what the hell was going on and he never let up either. Sometimes I felt like punching him in the mouth to make him shut up.

"Now, hush, Ed," said Minna. "That's all being taken care of."

"I just wanted to know what it was."

"It's incense," I said.

"What's incense?" asked Ed.

"Here it is," said Minna. She held up something wrapped in tissue paper and handed it to me. "I hope they fit."

It was a pair of white gloves with daisies embroidered on them. Thank God they were too small.

"Try them on," said Minna. "They look too small."

I tried them on and of course they were too small.

"What a pity," said Minna. "You got so big. I'll give them

to Nancy and get you the next size up. Forgive me, but you got so big."

"How about something to eat?" said Mother.

"That would be nice," said Ed. He still had his hat on.

"Go clean your room, Thelma," said Mother. (She had already put clean sheets on my bed and the extra bed in my room originally bought for sleep-over friends, but mostly used by either Minna or Ed. I never checked on who slept where.)

I went into my room and gathered up all the crap on the floor and threw everything into the bottom of my closet. It took longer than you would think. There was a lot of junk around. As I was dealing with all this junk I could hear the conversation in the other room.

Mother coming in with food tray.

"I didn't know what you wanted so I made tea and coffee and we have cookies and crumb buns and there's Jell-O in the kitchen."

"I want some," said Ed. "Some Jell-O'd be real nice."

"You don't need any Jell-O," said Minna. "Just hush now."

"She's got it, Minna. She just said so."

"It's no trouble," said my mother. "Anyone else want some while I'm going back to get some for Ed?"

"I'd like some," said my father, "if it's no trouble, if you're going back to get some for Ed."

"Two Jell-Os," said my mother. "Do you want some Jell-O, Minna?"

"No thanks," said Minna. "I had some yesterday."

"So did I," said Ed. "That's no reason. Have some more."

"I don't care for any more, thanks," said Minna. "I'm not that fond of Jell-O in the first place."

"You're not?" said Ed.

"No."

"You never told me that."
"Well, it's true."
"You had some yesterday."
"I know."
"Why'd you have some yesterday if you don't like it?"
"Hush, Ed."
"No, that's funny, isn't it? Eating something you don't like for no reason? I mean we weren't out or anything. We were at home. It wasn't as if you were being polite. It was right in our icebox. What'd you eat it for, Minna?"
"Never mind."
"No, I'm curious."
"Never mind."
"Don't you find that odd, Bill? A person sits right down in their own house, right there in their own kitchen and eats something they don't like. That's darn strange."
"I don't know," said my father.
"I mean it's coo-coo."
"Hush now, Ed."
"Here's the Jell-O," said my mother.
"Don't give any to Minna. She doesn't like it."
"That'll do, Edward."
"Darn strange if you ask me."
"Take off your hat."
"What?"
"Take off your hat. He always wears his hat inside. He never takes it off. If I didn't remind him he'd wear it to bed."
"Oh, I would not, Min."
"You certainly would. You'd wear it straight to bed. I always have to remind you."
"It doesn't matter," said Ed.
"Certainly it matters," said Minna. "It's not polite. You

know that. You know it as well as I do. A gentleman is supposed to take off his hat indoors. Ladies, hats on. Gents, hats off. He knows that. You know what, Ed? I wouldn't be surprised if you've lost your sense of feeling up there on top of your head. Maybe you just don't feel your hat up there. Your nerves may have gone numb or something. I'll bet it could happen. Maybe you just don't have any feeling up there so you can't sense your hat up there on your head."

"I just like to wear my hat."

That's a sample. They went on for some time, but it all sounded pretty much the same. I wanted to go to bed, but since my bed was the living room couch I was out of luck. I still had my headache and my knuckles hurt from smashing my fist into the wall. I went into the bathroom and took some aspirin and then headed for the kitchen. Whenever I felt really bad the only things that seemed to help were two aspirins followed by something chocolate, cake or brownies, ice cream, chocolate grahams, Mallomars, hot fudge, Milky Way bars, whatever. On my way through the living room to the kitchen Minna tried to stop me.

"Have a snack with us, sweetie," she said.

"I've got some stuff to do in the kitchen," I said, not stopping.

"Well, finish up and come on in here," she said. "We want to get a look at you."

I struck it rich in the chocolate department. There were chocolate donuts and Mallomars in the breadbox and ice cream in the freezer. I made myself a cup of tea while I ate some ice cream, and when the tea was ready I had that with a donut. Then I took the box of Mallomars out to the garage to share them with James.

CHAPTER EIGHT

The week dragged on. Kevin's rash wasn't any better. He had been to two doctors. One gave him some green cream to put on it. It was gross. Jennifer had stopped fainting although she had taken to vomiting. Maybe it was Kevin's green neck. Every time he came in she'd leave right away to throw up.

"I'm going to be sick," she'd say, and leave the room. One look was all it took. When she came back from throwing up she looked very pale and about five pounds thinner. (The Incredible Shrinking Sister.)

I was definitely flipping out. There was Jennifer's throwing up and Kevin's green neck and then my father was laid off from work. My mother got hysterical about that and the wedding arrangements which were interfered with by my father losing his job.

Then there was still Minna and Ed. I hadn't had a night's sleep in five days (nights). The first night it started. I waited up until after midnight so I'd be really tired and go right to sleep, but no such luck. The couch is the most uncomfortable thing to sleep on I've ever run into. I could not get to sleep. My back was killing me. There was no way to find a comfortable position. I tossed and turned. Every position was worse than the one before. Then I started itching all over like tiny hamsters were running through my veins. After forever I must have fallen asleep because I remember waking up and my pillow, my sheets and my blankets were all in a heap on the floor, except for one sheet which had my legs in a death grip. My back was throbbing. I was freezing. I got up and, after untangling my poor legs, staggered over and turned on the light and attempted to remake the couch as best I could. Then I fell back onto it and lapsed into a deep sleep, only to be awakened by my alarm. (I HATE THAT SOUND!) I leaned over to turn it off as usual and go back to sleep so my mother could have the pleasure of yelling at me to get up, when THERE WAS ED. He was sitting in the chair right next to me in his pajamas and his shoes and socks, staring into space. I wanted to scream. Every night it was the same and every morning there was Ed in his pajamas and shoes and socks. One morning he had his hat on. I could never be alone. I couldn't even shut myself in the bathroom because Jennifer would have to come in and throw up. I was flipping out and while I was flipping out I had to be right in the midst of crazy people, from school to the funny farm, with Ed in his pajamas and Minna talking and my father in the Grand Tune-out of all time and my mother hysterical and Jennifer throwing up and Kevin with his green neck.

I remember one morning in particular. I was sitting on the couch, unmade from the night before, reading *National Lampoon*, and my father was sitting nearby staring out the window (what else is new?). Minna came in and sat next to me on the couch and began talking.

"You're growing up so nice and big, sweetie. It seems like the last time I was here you were half this size, but that was only last spring."

It was hard to concentrate on my *National Lampoon* with her going on like that.

"You're not thin either. An undernourished person isn't attractive." (What did she think of Jennifer?)

My mother came in from the kitchen.

"How dare you sit on an unmade bed and read?"

"Couch," I muttered into my magazine. I don't think she heard me.

"Make it this minute!" She moved over to my father at the window. "WHAT ARE YOU DOING?"

He didn't answer. Sounds of Jennifer throwing up in the bathroom.

"Thelma's nice and firm," said Minna. "A thin person isn't attractive."

"THERE'S A WEDDING! I GET NO COOPERATION!" continued my mother. My father didn't seem to hear.

"Where's my toothbrush?" said Ed. He stood in the middle of the room wearing his hat, a raincoat, shoes and socks, with his pajama legs coming down from under his raincoat.

"Are you coming or going?" asked Minna. "You look mighty strange."

"Where's my toothbrush?"

"It must be in the bathroom. Don't go in there, though. Jennifer's not feeling well."

"What's the matter with her?"

"She's feeling a little queasy."

Sounds of Jennifer throwing up.

"I'll just ask her for my toothbrush."

"Leave her be."

"HELP ME DO SOMETHING!" said my mother to my father. "DO YOU HEAR ME AT ALL?"

Ed went over and rapped on the bathroom door.

"Where's my toothbrush?"

"Just a minute," Jennifer said feebly from inside the bathroom.

"Don't bother her, Ed. Hells bells."

"I just want my toothbrush."

"That can wait."

Jennifer came out of the bathroom. She held on to the door for balance. She looked like chalk.

"Is my toothbrush in there?"

"Look yourself, you big dummy," said Minna.

"I just want my toothbrush."

The doorbell rang.

"I'll get it," said my mother. "I have to do everything."

She opened the door and Kevin came in with a fresh application of cream on his neck. He looked like he'd been packed in avocado dip.

"Good morning," he said.

"Excuse me," said Jennifer, heading for the bathroom.

"I found it," said Ed.

"I'm going to be sick."

"I'm brushing my teeth."

"Let her in, Ed. Hells bells."

That was the gist. The only sane one around was James and he was out there in the North Pole.

Everything built up to the night before THE WEDDING. The thing that set off the time bomb, me, was getting kicked out of the house. Kevin was at home with his green neck and Jennifer was in the bathtub. It was about seven-thirty and my mother was rushing around the living room pushing things and dusting and setting out bowls of nuts. She was having the Cushmans and the Vincents in to wish Jennifer a happy wedding and to meet Minna and Ed. Minna was sitting over in the corner of the living room doing her nails (clear polish with just a tint of rose—"Buff Angel" I think it was called) and singing "Roll Out the Barrel" in this very nasal and LOUD VOICE. She did that a lot. She would sing loud and I mean LOUD, not just to herself like an ordinary human person, but LOUD like she was in a big theater and had to project to the second balcony.

"Roll out the barrel," sang Minna, "we'll have a barrel of fun. Roll out the barrel, we'll have a barrel of fun . . ."

"Maybe they don't like peanuts!" my mother said suddenly. She looked really upset and stood motionless, a bowl of peanuts in each hand, staring at the kitchen door.

"Roll out the barrel, we'll have a barrel of fun . . ."

"What else have I got? Chips!" said my mother, and went into the kitchen. Minna started up again.

"Roll out the barrel, we'll have a barrel of fun . . ."

Ed was taking a nap in my room. How he ever slept through Minna's concert I'll never know. Maybe he was just pretending to be asleep to get away from everything. I wouldn't blame him. I was hanging around waiting to get into the bathroom to get some aspirin. My head was splitting. I had already pounded on the door once, but Jennifer wouldn't let me in, the bitch. I tried again.

"Let me in for God's sake. All I want is an aspirin."

"Get the hell away from the door and leave me alone! Leave a person alone in the bathroom."

"Roll out the barrel, we'll have a barrel of fun . . ." She was off again.

"You knock on that door once more and I'll kill you!"

I went into the kitchen to check on the chocolate situation. My father was at the kitchen table with a bowl of chocolate ice cream melting in front of him. As usual he was staring out the window. My mother was up on a chair with her head inside one of the kitchen cupboards searching desperately for the potato chips. ("R-r-uffles have r-r-idges.")

"Did you eat the chips?" she snapped at me when I came in.

"I didn't touch the damn chips."

"I can do without the language, thank you. They were here yesterday."

"I didn't touch them."

There was no chocolate, only my father's ice cream melting before my eyes.

"Thank God!" said my mother. She grabbed a large bag of potato chips and headed back into the concert area.

Where could I go? I wanted to take a nap, a long nap, like maybe for a couple of weeks, but where? Ed was in my room, the couch—my bed—was in the center of the nut-and-chip distribution sector and soon would be the resting place for either Terry or Herb Vincent or Rosalie or Andrew Cushman or any combination of same. I thought of sleeping in the bathtub, but Jennifer's BIG SOAK made that impossible. What I did was lie down on the floor. My mother didn't take to it.

"Get off the floor, Thelma." (I hate that name. It is definitely the name of a homely person. Suitable to me, but why rub it in?) Anyway, my mother said, "Get off the floor, Thelma. We have company coming," but I didn't move. "Thelma, get up!"

I just lay there with my eyes shut tight and started counting to five hundred.

"Get up!"

Minna stopped singing "Roll Out the Barrel." (Thank God for small favors.) She said that maybe I was sick because I looked kind of funny.

"Nonsense," said my mother. "There's nothing wrong with her."

"She looks kind of funny to me."

"Nonsense. I know my own daughter. Get up!" she screamed at me. "Do you hear me??? Don't you know we have PEOPLE COMING OVER??? How dare you do this????"

I didn't feel good and I was comfortable there in spite of my mother screaming at me. I wanted to see how far this could go. One member of the family wants to stretch out on the floor and relax—what could this develop into? More than I bargained for! My mother started screaming even louder and said if I didn't get up this minute she was going to call the police. Just then Ed came out of MY ROOM.

"What's going on?" he said.

"We're having a disciplinary problem with Thelma," said my mother.

"THELMA!!!" It was Ed, screaming in my ear. "YOUR MOTHER WANTS YOU TO GET OFF THE FLOOR!"

"Don't scream at her, Ed," said Minna. "She looks kind of funny."

"Something's funny. I screamed right in her ear and she didn't even jump. Did you see that?"

"Go back and take a nap," said Minna.

Just then Jennifer came out of the bathroom and started screaming, "IF SHE EMBARRASSES ME TONIGHT OR AT THE WEDDING TOMORROW I'LL KILL HER. I CAN'T STAND IT ANYMORE!" Then she came over and grabbed me by the foot and started trying to drag me somewhere—I don't think she had thought of where. "GET UP, THELMA! GET UP! GET OUT OF HERE NOW OR I'LL KILL YOU!!!"

But she was weak from not eating and throwing up and she could hardly budge me.

"What's the matter with her?" said Ed. "I screamed right in her ear and she didn't even jump. What's wrong with her?"

"SHUT UP," said Jennifer. "YOU DON'T KNOW WHAT'S GOING ON!"

"Jennifer, that's uncalled for," said mother. "There's no need to scream at Ed."

"I CAN'T STAND IT ANYMORE," said Jennifer. "SHE'S RUINING MY LIFE!"

Jennifer ran, crying, from the room. Then the doorbell rang. It was the Cushmans. They came in and were introduced to Minna and Ed.

"Don't step on Thelma," said Ed, "she's right there on the floor."

"We're having a little problem with Thelma this evening," said my mother. "You know teenagers."

"Oh, dear, yes," said Rosalie. She seemed really confused, like she was afraid to step anywhere for fear of stepping on me. She backed up and Andrew grabbed her by the elbow.

He steered her toward the couch.

"Here we go, Rosalie," he said.

Then my father came in.

"Don't step on Thelma," said Ed. "She's lying on the floor."

"Oh, my," said my father.

"Did she have a toothache?" Rosalie asked unexpectedly.

"No. Nothing," said Ed. "She just ate dinner and that was that."

"Maybe it was the food," said Minna.

"Oh," said Rosalie. "I thought maybe she had a toothache because I had a friend in college once who had a toothache and fainted."

"That's ridiculous, Rosalie," said Andrew. "It could be anything. Why say it's a toothache? That's dumb."

They tried ignoring me. They discussed my father's job layoff and the opening of a new shopping mall in Rutherford, but then the Vincents came in and the whole thing started up again. I was getting a kick out of the whole scene when my mother started in on "Youth Today" and what would become of the world when we grew up, she hated to think. I was a trial, but then weren't all teenagers although of course Jennifer was the exception—never an ounce of trouble, thank the good Lord for her. (Why couldn't I be like Jennifer? Fainting and vomiting and marrying a sadistic fool for reasons I knew not of. Life was strange.)

Both the Vincents and the Cushmans agreed. The Cushmans' son, Robert Cushman, had let his hair grow to his waist and the Vincents had no teenagers yet, although they dreaded it from what they had heard. Their oldest was twelve and had asthma and they had friends whose daughter had died from taking drugs and alcohol mixed and it was no picnic for them. How about another round of scotch and sodas?

"You're all a bunch of shits," I said.

"Get out of this house!" screamed my mother. "And stay out until you can behave like a human being!"

I grabbed my pea jacket from off the doorknob of the hall closet and left, slamming the door. I remember laughing. These poor miserable slobs, their empty lives filled with details they detest, jobs they hate, families they don't even know. They drink their way through their lives, coffee till five, scotch and soda till midnight, they bow down to their god, money, then inflation turns overnight into a depression and they're left flat on their asses. How can they be so dense? How dare they criticize those who question them? I was hysterical with laughter—high on rage. I found myself in the garage and there was James, staring up at me and the minute I looked at him I fell apart. I started sobbing and shaking and I couldn't stop. I got down on my knees and put my arms around him and just kept on crying. He tried to lick my face. I always talk to him, but I was crying too hard to talk. I had trouble getting my breath and I thought, if only I could stop crying I could breathe again, but I just kept on. I don't know how long it was. Later, maybe a half hour, an hour, two hours, I don't know, I lay down on the cold cement floor with my arms around James and just stayed like that for a long time. I was breathing easier, a little anyway, and I wasn't choking. Tears were just coming down silently and I had to breathe with my mouth open (my lips were so chapped). Then I started getting mad again. HOW DARE THEY? I had to get up and I started pacing around, talking to myself. Jimmy looked up at me like I was crazy.

"HOW DARE THEY? HOW DARE THEY???!!! WHO DO THEY THINK THEY ARE??? WHAT DO THEY WANT ME TO DO??? WHERE DO THEY WANT ME TO GO??? WHY DIDN'T I TURN OUT LIKE JENNIFER? I DON'T WANT TO BE LIKE JENNIFER!! I'D RATHER BE DEAD!!!"

This is very hard for me to write. (Are you there, Dr. Stone?) It's been easy up to now. I don't know if it's clear, or interesting, but all the stuff wanted to come out. I would come up to the rec hall with my yellow pad or sometimes work right in my "House" living room, or my bedroom, but I would just sit down and write and write. Now I don't want to write and if I make myself sit down to begin in an effort to recapture the former exhilaration writing brought me I don't want to begin. Well, I'll begin anyway.

CHAPTER NINE

I found myself walking. I remember telling Jim that I had to take a walk, I'd see him later. I don't know why I didn't take him with me. As it turned out it would have complicated things, but I couldn't have known what I was about to do. Or could I?

I walked, still crying, but silently now, and I remember feeling SO SAD AND SO LONELY AND SO UNLOVED —and SO ANGRY. I talked to myself a lot as if I was talking to one of them.

I found myself passing the Ethical Culture building, almost like a house, white, with a sign saying ETHICAL CULTURE SOCIETY out front. Why was I there? I know now, of course, but I didn't then.

I stared at the building. Rage welled up in me. I felt like screaming. I walked around the white building, loathing its every timber. I'd like to burn the damn thing down, I remember thinking. That'd put off the wedding. Or maybe not. (I pictured a wedding ceremony complete with gown and train and corsage amidst black ash and fallen timbers and me in my Snoopy sweat shirt up on a half-broken rafter taking pictures with my Polaroid 220.) I started laughing and then crying and then I was doing both at once. I sat down with my back against a big maple tree (Maplewood, New Jersey after all). It was freezing cold. I could see my breath, white and foggy as it came out of my mouth. The moon was bright. It was a clear night with lots of stars. My hands were freezing, and I didn't have any gloves, so I put them into my pockets. There was a book of matches in my pocket. I took out the matches and lit one. It burned down and I was still crying. I lit another one.

I should touch this flame to the building, I thought. It would be simple. Stop the wedding. Start from scratch. Purify the air.

Then, so simply, I got up and walked over to the building and lit another match. I had stopped crying. I held the match to the underside of the wooden window ledge and let it burn. It made a black mark on the wood but nothing caught. I tried it again, still it didn't catch. It's not so easy to burn down a building, I remember thinking. If I were really trying to burn this building down I wouldn't have such an easy time of it. I tried it again and again and still nothing happened. There was just this row of black marks on the window ledge. I guess you have to use another, smaller piece of wood. A branch, I remember deciding. I went to look for one, forgetting for the moment the distinction between burning down a building and figuring how I would do it if I were going to do it. I found a branch and brought it back to the building. Then I lit the branch, which was long. This time I tried one of the shutters. I lit the branch and held it right by the shutter. I can put it out if it catches, I figured. It caught and the strange thing was, I was paralyzed. I just didn't move to put out the fire. I just stood, watching it. When it got too hot I backed up and kept watching. The flames went up the shutter and across the window ledge (that part caught at last) and then up the other shutter. It wasn't too long before the basic building itself started to burn and I just stood, watching it. I heard voices and screaming and then lots of people started gathering around. I'll leave. It doesn't belong to me anymore. It's theirs now, and I walked away. I walked a few blocks and fire engines came. They sped by me toward the fire with bells ringing and sirens going.

I walked a lot that night. I went down to the railroad station and sat there for a while. Then I walked some more. Around six in the morning I passed the police station. It looked cozy inside, cozy and warm—lights on, people there. I sat down on the pavement with my back against the building, my teeth chattering and me shivering all over. After a while I went in. (Perhaps I wanted to be caught. What would you say, Dr. Stone? That is, if you talked.)

It was warm inside the police station and I sat down. Some lady next to me didn't have any shoes on and her legs were all puffed up and blue. She was crying. Pretty soon a policeman came over and took her into another room. A policeman asked me if he could help me, but I didn't answer.

"What are you doing here?" he asked.

"Nothing," I said.

"You should be home in bed," he said.

I didn't say anything.

"Where do you live?"

I didn't answer.

"What's your address?"

I started crying.

"Come with me," he said, real bored, like he'd already said it two thousand times that same night and he didn't want to fill out another form. He took me into a small room with paint coming off the wall and a light bulb hanging from the ceiling. There was a desk and a couple of chairs and a small bookshelf with papers and stuff. It was messy and dark and very cold.

The policeman sat behind the desk and told me to sit in the other chair. He picked up the phone and asked me what my phone number was. I didn't answer.

"Come on now, kid. All I want is your phone number. I'm not going to bite you." I still didn't say anything.

"What's your phone number?!" He said it louder and slower and more distinctly this time like he thought maybe I was deaf or retarded or spoke another language. (Latin, maybe?)

"Look, kid, you just can't sit around here. You either leave and go home or wherever you want to go, I don't care, or you tell me your phone number and I'll have somebody come down here and pick you up. You can't just sit around, O.K.? You want some coffee?" (That drink again.)

I was freezing and starving and half awake and a cup of coffee sounded pretty good to me. I nodded.

"O.K., we'll get you a nice hot cup of coffee, you drink it down and then you tell me your phone number and I'll call up your folks and have them come down here and get you. Are you all right?" I was still crying. "You're not hurt or anything, are you?"

I didn't respond, so he left the room and came back with

this watery coffee in this Styrofoam cup with maybe a drop or two of skimmed milk in it. There wasn't any sugar. But I drank it anyway. He left the room for a while and then came back with another policeman. The first policeman was thin with glasses and a moon-shaped face and yellow fingers (I guess from smoking). Anyway, one policeman was thin with yellow fingers (he ought to meet Kevin with his green neck) and the other was humongous, like some kind of homely Roman god of muscle.

"O.K., so what's your phone number?" said the one with the yellow fingers. "Let's have it."

When I didn't answer the humongous one moved forward.

"Listen, kid, this ain't no hotel. You can't stay here. This is a place of business. We are involved here in various and sundry matters pertaining to your public citizen." (Not mine!) "You gotta go."

When I didn't move or say anything they left. They didn't come back for an hour or so, and when they did come back they took me to another room that was smaller and darker and colder than the first.

"Think it over," said the policeman with the yellow fingers, and they left. I don't know how long I was in there for, two or three hours or something. After a while thoughts started going through my head which was new because up until then they really hadn't (been?). I could see the fire before my eyes, closed or open (my eyes, that is); it didn't seem to matter, and then I kept picturing my family and wondering what they were doing over my disappearance. Nothing was my first thought—the worst—they were doing nothing—just sleeping peacefully in their beds. Then I started thinking of other things. Wishes? (Are you there,

Dr. Stone?) My father walking around the yard in his bathrobe and pajamas, calling my name, my mother calling friends, parents of friends, to see if I might be there. Jonathan Bessmer would know nothing nor would Penny, or any of the others. Jennifer would be too busy drying her hair or throwing up and I didn't much care what Minna and Ed were doing. Then I had a picture that gave me the chills! My mother calling the police station to see if they knew where I was. She might do that, or was that wishful thinking? DUMB! Why did I come here? Did I want to be found?

After the LONGEST TIME five policemen came into the room. I knew right away there was trouble and I guess I knew the whole nature of it, everything. A young girl had been seen hanging around the Ethical Culture building before the fire and she looked like me (or I looked like her) and the policemen were all upset. There were two women outside who claimed to have seen this girl and the policemen wanted to know where I was all night. I didn't answer for the longest time, but I was getting so hungry and so tired and I didn't care anymore. I didn't care about anything. Only stopping the hunger pain in my stomach, and going to sleep.

"WERE YOU IN THE VICINITY OF THE MAPLEWOOD ETHICAL CULTURE SOCIETY AT ANY TIME THIS EVENING?"

"Yes." (It was true, it was the answer they wanted and maybe they would leave me alone and let me sleep.)

"WHAT WERE YOU DOING THERE?"

"Setting fire to it." (Again the truth, somewhere a seed of curiosity. How would they take that?)

One of the policemen snapped his fingers and pointed to another policeman who ran out and came back with this man with a pad. He didn't have a uniform on, but I supposed he was a policeman.

"Name?" said the man.

"Thelma Beldwin." I didn't care, cared nothing about what happened to me. If I answered their questions maybe I could have a nap or a sandwich.

"Address?"

"Sixty-two Pinetree Road."

"Telephone number?"

"Six-two-nine—eight-five-three-one."

"Tell us everything that happened."

"When?"

"What did you do at the Ethical Culture Society?"

"I set fire to it."

That was obviously not enough for them. They wanted all the gory details. This is what they put up with the boredom of their lives for, moments like this, well, moments like this and the money, although I don't suppose they make much money doing what they do. (Tending to the various and sundry matters pertaining to your public citizen as he so succinctly put it.) I don't imagine that kind of tending pays very well—no—they must mostly wait for the gory details of various and sundry crimes. That must be what gets them through. Well, damned if I'd make their day.

"Tell us everything that happened."

"I don't want to."

"You have to. We're police officers. Tell us in your own words what happened."

It was like I was encased in a thin gauze bandage. Everything had this unreal quality.

"Why did you go to the Ethical Culture Society?"

"I don't know."

"You must know. Did you approach the building with intent to set fire to it?"

"I don't know."

"You must know. Did you approach the building with intent to set fire to it?"

"I don't think so."

"You approached the building and what happened? What did you do?"

"I set fire to it."

"Why did you do that?"

"I don't know."

"You don't know why you set fire to the Ethical Culture Society? You must have a reason!"

No answer.

"What did you do after you set the fire?"

"I left."

"Call the parents," said my old friend with the yellow fingers. I can remember thinking, Maybe now I can get some sleep, but they brought the women who said they had seen me into the room and they looked at me and both said I was me. I could have told them that. Then the policeman who had asked me all the questions (I don't remember what he looked like) said, "Wait here," and everybody left. I don't know how much time went by after that because I fell asleep.

It's weird how hard it's getting for me to write this. (Hi, Dr. Stone.) Anyway, it's suddenly HARD. What I'm up to now is my parents coming to get me at the precinct (sounds like movie or T.V. talk). Anyway, they did come and after that was THE WEDDING AND THE RECEPTION just as though nothing had happened—well, almost. I think that was the worst part of it. I did this MONU-

MENTAL, HORRENDOUS THING and everything just continued along. I hardly made a dent!! It enrages me even today and I'm verging on sanity (right, Dr. Stone? You never tell me ANYTHING—just listen with your big all-encompassing ears and your dark-rimmed glasses).

ANYWAY, when I woke up my parents were coming into the room with the original policeman, the one with the yellow fingers. The policeman was saying "There she is," and I lifted my head from where it was resting on my arms on the desk and there they were, all dressed up for the wedding. It was weird. My father didn't say anything (as usual), but the most AMAZING AND UNHEARD-OF THING was that my mother didn't say anything either—at first. My mother speechless!

The policeman with the yellow fingers told me to come with them, so I got up and followed them out of the room and down the hall and into this other, bigger room. It had two desks and several chairs. We all sat down and the policeman talked. It seems that "my fire" was very unsubstantial. It got just part of the building—one wall was damaged and inside there was a lot of smoke, and everything there was really messed up a lot, but not too much was destroyed, just part of a wall, as I said. It wasn't going to be too much of a deal to repair it, but they couldn't have any weddings there for a couple of days, so THE WEDDING was switched to the Rutherford branch. BIG DEAL! Everything seemed pitiful and hopeless, especially changing life or anything like that. I was what they called "released in my parents' custody pending a hearing," and then everybody would decide what to do with me. I didn't care. I just wanted some soup, or a sandwich or a bowl of shredded wheat.

CHAPTER TEN

Now what is the most incredible part of the whole business is what happened next. Because of having to switch THE WEDDING to a different branch (sounds like a tree), a branch which takes at least forty-five minutes to get to, and because of the extra pressures to the schedule of Ethical Culture due to the "mishap," we were almost late for THE WEDDING. It was originally set for 2:00 P.M. in Maplewood, but now it would be 1:00 P.M. in Rutherford and that made everything rushed. Of course there was the TERRIBLE CATASTROPHE of having "time to kill" between THE WEDDING at 1:00 P.M. and THE RECEPTION at 3:30 P.M., but right now the thing of UTMOST IMPORTANCE seemed to be getting to Rutherford. Jennifer had already gone over with Minna and Ed and we were to meet them there. I was still expected to go to the wedding. And here is the single weirdest thing. My parents had brought my blouse and jumper to the police station and I was supposed to change there. I mean that was so weird, changing in that obnoxious, filthy ladies room at the police station to go to the wedding. I felt like Joan of Arc, whom I connect with deeply. One thing that drove them wild during her trial was that she refused to wear a dress. I love that! There she is in chains in that grungy prison all alone except for the guards who torture her and the trial guys get this thing about what she's wearing. Putting aside the fact that it was February and freezing in that prison tower (no central heating) and the guards were trying to rape her, putting aside these reasonable reasons for selecting pants instead of a dress, what possible difference could it make what the cut of her wardrobe was? People are CRAZY!!! Another thing that drove them wild at the trial was that she gave instructions to men, like in the battles and everything, she, a lowly woman, told MEN what to do. SHE DIDN'T KNOW HER PLACE! The thing was she knew precisely her place. They didn't know her place, but they didn't know they didn't know it. Anyway, not to equate myself with her, it's that I couldn't help thinking of her in there in that dingy police station. I wasn't allowed to see the light of day, to walk out of there with my parents, never mind having soup and a sandwich (which were uppermost to me then) until I put on a dress. It's funny what matters to people. It didn't matter to my parents that my sister was that very day being locked into matrimony with someone she didn't like or love and who didn't respect her as a human person. What mattered was that I should wear a dress.

My father went out to the car and got my jumper and blouse and brought them back to the police station and I took them, along with instructions to wash my hands and face (my mother's first words to me), and went into the ladies room. I put on the jumper and washed my face and hands like a good girl because I no longer cared about anything. Going against my parents' wishes, sticking up for what I believed in, being true to myself, or anyone else for that matter, nothing held any appeal for me. Eating and going to sleep, that was all.

I came out of the ladies room, wearing my jumper and carrying my jeans, and my mother gave me a comb and told me to comb my hair. I did and we left. The car was parked across the street and we got in (me in the back, my father driving. My mother never drives when my father's in the car. "Women don't" I think is the reason), and we started our drive to Rutherford. I fell asleep.

When the car stopped at Ethical Culture I woke up right away. Jennifer was coming toward the car.

"Thank God you're here," she said. "It's five to one."

My father didn't know where to park and my mother said she would get out and he should park up the street.

"Hurry!" said Jennifer.

Mother and I got out of the car and went inside.

Please let there be hors d'oeuvres, I prayed, *before* the ceremony. But there was nothing because it was already starting.

"Congratulations," people said to mother. "How beautiful Jennifer looks!"

They said what a shame it was about the fire, everything having to be changed at the last minute, but thank God no one was hurt. The ceremony began. There were about twenty-five people. Kevin stood up front with the Ethical Culture Man and my father came in with Jennifer. She did look gorgeous (the bitch!) although TENSE, all white and pasty looking. My father was in a daze. He had good reason with one daughter getting married and the other burning down buildings and his own last-minute difficulty in finding a parking place. But since he's always in a daze, that's no excuse. The Ethical Culture Man gave a speech about how they should respect each other as people (Jennifer and Kevin??) and help each other grow as individuals.

It was really like a dream. I kept thinking of the Holiday Inn and THE RECEPTION and FOOD! Everybody kissed everybody and cried and said the wedding couldn't have been nicer. I've never felt so alone. I had been through this whole big thing and even the ones who knew were ignoring it and me. It was like not existing.

We got to the Holiday Inn in Montclair one hour before THE RECEPTION was due to begin, but miraculously the party was set up. Nuts, crackers and cheese and tiny sandwiches were just inside the entrance door. Paradise! I also had five Cokes.

There was a row of tables along one wall that had all the drinks and hors d'oeuvres and there were sitting-down tables with name cards and a dance floor. The band played the theme from *Love Story* and "If Ever I Would Leave You" from *Camelot*. It was touching. I saw no sign of Jennifer's dear friend Marge with the lovely froglike voice. (Remember Kevin's pigheaded veto of her medley of show tunes?) I didn't expect her anyway. I stood by the hors d'oeuvres table, eating. Rosalie Cushman came by (remember—sunbaths through November?). It seems she hadn't eaten all day which caused her to giggle and reach out for the nuts. She looked very dark, her skin I mean. If I hadn't known better I would have assumed she was black, or brown to be more exact. ("The blacks" should be called "the browns" if you're looking for any sort of descriptive phrase. Personally, I'm not. It's weird to lump people into groups according to physical characteristics. You don't call people with blond hair "the lights" or big feet "the bigs." It makes no sense. But if it's done, one might as well be accurate. The only person I've seen with black skin is Rosalie Cushman and she's "white.")

Rosalie reached out for the nuts and I headed for my place at the table. I was so tired I was ready to fall on my face. The band was playing the theme from *The Godfather* and lots of people were dancing.

I was seated next to Mrs. Pavlo, the mother of Jennifer's best friend, Leslie. Mrs. Pavlo was staring off into space when I sat down. She smiled at me.

"What a lovely reception," she said.

I just kept on eating my hors d'oeuvres. I didn't answer. I didn't smile. I didn't have the strength. Pretty soon Mr. Pavlo sat down along with a lady with a limp and a big bowl of fruit salad. Mrs. Pavlo smiled her big smile and Mr. Pavlo started complaining about the rotten food.

"That's just hors d'oeuvres," said Mrs. Pavlo. "They'll bring your main dish. They have waiters."

"If it's anything like the hors d'oeuvres I don't want it."

"Be nice."

"Be nice yourself. The food stinks."

"Now, Sid."

"It stinks. Your brain's melting."

"Somebody got up on the wrong side of the bed."

"I wonder who that could be," said Mr. Pavlo, and left the table.

Mrs. Pavlo turned to the lady with the fruit salad and the limp. "He's just grouchy today because he wanted to shoot a turkey."

"Oh, my."

"He heard about some wild turkeys upstate and he wanted to go up and shoot one. I made him come to this."

I know how it is when you want to go out and kill something and then you can't. It ruins your day.

"He'll get over it," continued Mrs. Pavlo. "He always does."

"Oh, sure."

"So how have you been?"

"Fine."

"I haven't seen you for weeks."

"It seems like ages."

"You cut your hair."

"It's too short."

"I like it."

"I don't."

"What have you been up to?" asked Mrs. Pavlo.

"We put in a new kitchen."

"Wonderful."

"It's open."

"An open kitchen."

"I love it."

"I have one."

"You do?"

"Sure."

"They knocked out three walls."

"You poor thing."

"But it's worth it."

"Of course."

"You know what I love about an open kitchen?"

"What?"

"You're not alone."

"It's true."

"The woman is always stuck in the kitchen."

"Of course."

"But now there's not that terrible loneliness. I can talk to my family while I work."

"Or your guests for that matter."

"Or my guests."

(Gloria Steinem, you may not be all that bad.)

Every few minutes these flames would flare up in front of my eyes—memory of the fire—and I'd be almost falling asleep. I've never been that tired, before or since.

"Did you hear about the fire?" asked Mrs. Pavlo.

"I did," said the fruit-limp lady. "Wasn't it awful?"

"They had to rearrange everything."

"And on such short notice."

"Awful."

"How did it happen?"

"Some kid started it."

"That doesn't surprise me."

"Me either."

"A boy?"

"A girl."

"Drunk, I suppose."

"It wouldn't surprise me."

"Me either. The drinking problem is terrible you know. It's not the drugs so much. The new thing is liquor."

"Not new."

"Well, not new, but a change from the drugs."

"A change, of course. Thank God I don't have teenagers anymore," said Mrs. Pavlo. "It's such a worry."

"I have a teenage son," said the fruit-limp lady. "I'm in

agony all the while."

Right then they both noticed me with my five Cokes and my nuts and empty sandwich plate.

"What is it with you kids?" asked the fruit-limp lady. "You put us through the tortures of the damned, but we love you."

I had another few nuts and didn't answer. They forgot about me and went on to discuss the teenage drinking problem. There was an awful lot of it in Maplewood, although I can't stand the stuff. It makes me nauseous. I guess that's a lucky break because crazy as I was (and still am to a degree—don't get pompous!) I probably would have tucked it away pretty good what with peer pressure and all. Up here at NWS there's some drinking, but not as much. I guess there's not as much shit under the surface—everything's out in the open more (hello, Dr. Stone) so our craziness doesn't need to come out in oblique ways. There is some drinking and quite a bit of pot, which I like although I don't like to talk about it. I feel like some policeman will leap out from around a corner of my desk and put me away for possession. I love my paranoid seizures. Now I'm getting away from pot because of meditation. Meditation is a better high for me than marijuana, so marijuana is falling away from my life, but more of that later.

For now we are here at THE RECEPTION at the Holiday Inn and I'm viewing it behind gauze. "Released in parents' custody pending a hearing." Me? That was television news talk, nothing for a short, brainless, scatterbrained neurotic troll like myself.

Then a terrible thing happened. The lady with the fruit salad and the limp DISREGARDED THE PLACECARDS

AND SAT WHERE SHE DIDN'T BELONG. What an embarrassing situation. She now had to be asked to move! With her limp and her half-finished bowl of fruit. It was too much! My mother had to do it since the POOR LADY was sitting in Minna's place and Minna now wanted to sit down. Everything got straightened out, thank God! And Minna sat down with a glass of orange juice and Ed not far behind.

"We were so worried about you, Thelma," said Minna, taking my hand and looking deeply into my eyes. "What happened? Are you all right?"

"I guess so," I said.

"You look tired."

"I am tired."

"Well, you look tired. Doesn't she look tired, Ed?"

"Yes," said Ed. He was just sitting down with his humongous plate of food and of course his hat was on.

About then this couple that I loathe sat down. They aren't close with my parents, but my mother would like them to be. They have more money than most of the folks in Maplewood and they're "Live Wires," Sparky and Sylvia Davis. He works in television and she plays tennis and reads. I once heard her confess to my mother that "you can play only so much tennis and then you wonder what life is all about." Right on, Sylvia! Anyway, they sat down. Sparky Davis (Did his parents give him that name?) started making dumb jokes and was drinking like a fish. He said Jennifer was "some tomato," just like his daughter Joey who had a "great bod." Revolting! Especially for a father to talk that way about his own daughter. Joey wouldn't see a thing wrong in her father talking like that about her. She worships him.

The rest of the reception is a blur. There was more food

and Ed with his hat on, and Sparky and Sylvia and my nervous and hysterical mother, my vacant-eyed father, Jennifer and Kevin cutting the cake, Jennifer and Kevin dancing, Jennifer and Kevin kissing, Jennifer and Kevin thanking people who wished them all the happiness in the world, Kevin's parents viewing my parents with suspicious disdain, the band playing "My Funny Valentine" and "The Mexican Hat Dance," Mrs. Pavlo passing out with her nose in her salad, Mr. Pavlo walking out before the cake was served and me going into the lobby and falling asleep on one of the couches.

CHAPTER ELEVEN

The next two weeks were like death. I was waiting for "them" to decide what to do with me. I couldn't eat and started losing all this weight. The thought of food made me want to puke. I had a terrible headache and my sinuses puffed up and my eyes were tiny, red and piglike. I stayed in bed mostly, or in my pajamas at least. I didn't care if I lived or died and knew that no one else cared either. I didn't know what I should do. It was freezing and with me feeling so rotten I didn't see Jimmy once. I feel terrible about that still. If I'd had the presence of mind to go out and see him he might have helped me, but I didn't.

It was a weird time. Jennifer was gone. My parents seemed lost (more than usual that is) without her. Really depressed. My father was around the house all the time, wondering what to do. I have vague memories of him in a gray cardigan, sitting and staring into space, making himself toast and Campbell's soup. One day, he came into my bedroom. His cardigan was buttoned lopsided, on the wrong buttons, which gave me the creeps.

"Hi there," he said. "I'm about to make myself some soup."

That was all he said for a while. I stared at the ceiling. I thought he'd leave and I wouldn't see him for hours, or days, but after a minute or two he said, "Would you like some chicken gumbo?"

"Don't talk to me about soup," I said, "or I'll throw up."

"Oh," he said, and left my room. He never mentioned food to me again.

I stayed in my room and listened to my James Taylor records and watched T.V. I remember a commercial. This airline claimed they were doing what they did best. I remember that they never told you what it was that they did. You might not want it done.

To add to the horror of that time, two girls I knew were killed in an automobile accident. Both had been drinking, but neither was driving and the kid who was driving hadn't been drinking. It was so strange. They drove into a tree and that was that. The kid who was driving was O.K. and another kid in the car, a guy, just broke his hip, but these girls were both killed. I didn't know them well, but they were in several of my classes at school. A week before the wedding another kid had been killed in a car crash. He was driving alone and drunk. I understood it in an odd kind of way. We don't really value our own lives. Most of the kids in Maplewood were unhappy and felt insignificant (me included!), but along with this feeling that we were insignificant we had this overblown opinion of ourselves. Nothing could happen to us. We were beyond it. Above and below. I was the same way. It could have been me except I was too busy being crazy in other ways.

Another weird thing about that time was how my parents ignored me. More than usual. My father, well it's hard to tell with him. I believe he was ignoring everything in general and me in particular. After all, I did set fire to a building. Someone else's building and I had no right to do that. It's a big thing. Worthy of a comment, a mention, a question, a reprimand at least, but nothing did I get. My mother was even stranger. She actively ignored me. Silent disdain. She brought me food on a tray that I would look at and get nauseous from. She once brought me a doctor.

"Hello, little lady," he said, coming through the door with his satchel of goodies. He was the smallest full-grown person I've ever seen except in the circus. He looked about four feet tall. Was he a midget? "I've never seen you before," he said. "I'm covering."

Covering what?

"Let's have a look. Unbutton your pajama top there."

He put his stethoscope under my minute left breast.

"Let's have a listen."

He listened to my heart, took my blood pressure with his wonderful collapsing vein machine, looked in my mouth, my ears, my eyes, took my temperature (orally, thank the good Lord) and said there was nothing wrong with me. A lot he knew.

The days dragged on. Possibilities seemed to shrivel. It wasn't possible to go out because it was freezing and I was sick and I might get sicker. It wasn't possible to eat because I'd throw up. It wasn't possible to go into another room because my father would probably be there staring into space with his soup and his toast and his sweater and I'd want to cry. It wasn't possible to call Jonathan or Penny or anybody else and ask them to come over because they probably wouldn't want to or their mothers wouldn't want them to because they might catch my sickness. Also I didn't want anyone to see me because I looked so awful with my pig eyes and dirty hair. My hair had been dirty already on the night of the fire and after that I didn't care about washing it and my mother wasn't speaking to me so she couldn't make me wash it. I looked too awful to want to see anybody, or shall we say, have anybody see me, so visits were out. Nothing was possible.

Then one day Penny came over with a lemon meringue pie. Remember Penny? The girl who was always happy going to the movies or vacuuming the house? The one I was so suspicious of?

It was about four on a Thursday afternoon and the doorbell rang and it was Penny with this lemon meringue pie. My mother let her in and led her right into my room so I didn't have a chance to hide.

"Someone's here to see you," said my mother.

There was Penny with this pie and I took one look at her and started to cry. It was such a nice thing to do. Somebody had thought of me and done something nice for me. It was so nice and I couldn't eat it. I wanted more than anything in the world right then to be able to eat that pie, to show how grateful I was that somebody was nice to me.

"I brought you this lemon meringue pie," she said. "Where should I put it?"

"I'll take it," I said. She gave me the pie and I sat there in my pajamas on my bed holding it while she stood on one foot with the other foot pressed against her ankle.

"I made one for us too," she said. "It came out fantastic."

"Thank you," I said. "That's so nice of you."

"Oh, that's O.K.," she said. "I can't stay. I'm baby-sitting for the Rislers and Mrs. Risler is so particular you wouldn't believe it. I can't be five minutes late and you know, you won't believe this, if I have to make dinner or cook anything she writes this list. Water on stove in medium-sized pot. Turn on heat under pot to five. Take spoon from lower left-hand drawer. I mean I've baby-sat for her for over a year. She must think I'm a retard. She's nice though. Well, I'll see you later. I hope you feel better."

She left and I sat there holding this lemon meringue pie and crying. What a sweet girl.

About now I lose my sense of time. If I check on a calendar I can see that this period of bedridden despair lasted about two weeks. It seemed like an eternity. You don't know when you're in the middle of something like that when it will end, or if it will end. I just knew I was dying.

After about two weeks there was this hearing. I guess there had been lots of phone calls and meetings between my parents and lawyers and juvenile people (not children, that is, grown-ups who work with young delinquents) and court officials and Ethical Culture people and everything, but finally there was this hearing that I had to go to with my parents and there were these men there (no ladies). I was still in this sort of fog. I had gotten right out of my p.j.'s. and into that jumper I knew and loved so well.

Everyone else was there when we arrived. Four men, I think. A judge, a social worker, an Ethical Culture Man and someone from a board of something. The Ethical Culture Man wore a brown suit and sat by himself in a corner by the window.

"We're not in favor of pressing charges here," he said when the judge asked for his position. "Our recommendation is for psychological help for Thelma, perhaps a special school where she could have continuity of treatment."

"We're in accord," said the social worker. He looked like he'd just stepped out of the shower. His hair was wet. "We have information on several schools that have had great success in dealing with cases like these."

I'd become a case. Of what, I wondered.

"Private, or state funded?" asked the Board Man.

"Either," said the social worker.

"The private schools are extremely costly," said the Board Man.

"What are your feelings?" the judge asked my father.

"Private," said my mother. "We'd prefer to pursue the private."

"What are your feelings, Mr."—the judge consulted his papers—"Beldwin."

"Private," said my mother. She wouldn't let up. Social climbing in juvenile delinquent circles. Is there no stopping her?

"Mr. Beldwin?"

"We'll see what what we can do," said my father. He didn't seem to care.

"There are alternatives," said the judge. He had trouble opening his eyes. They were like slits, all puffy around the sides. Worse than mine. Had he been crying, or drinking too much scotch?

"We'll pursue the private," said Mother.

"Mr. Beldwin is presently unemployed, is he not?" asked the social worker. I could smell the Dial soap across the room. "Won't tuition be a burden?"

"We have many loving relatives who would be only too glad to assist should such a thing become necessary," said Mother. (She meant Minna and Ed.)

"I see," said the social worker.

"Then you'll pursue this course of action," said the judge. "You'll remain in contact with Mr. Bissim" (the shower king) "and he in turn will report to me. Thank you."

I didn't say a word. Nobody asked for my opinion. (Do cases talk?) I didn't have one anyway.

We went back home and I took off my jumper and got back into my pajamas and into bed. I lay there with a splitting headache, the room spinning around, and I started crying again. I realized I hadn't stopped in the garage to see my dear dog, James. My last link with the world, with caring for anyone, or anything. I had forgotten all about him. Surely this was the end.

THE BEGINNING

CHAPTER ONE

It was decided that I should go to North Woods School. It was small, with a sense of family and an excellent record of helping "people like me." It was in Vermont and very expensive. I found out later that Minna and Ed had offered to help with tuition which is probably the only way I could have gone. I'm glad they made that offer, God bless them. This place has helped me a lot, although I still have a way to go.

By that time it was mid-December, so it seemed that I would be "sent away" at the end of Christmas vacation to start the winter term. Some lady would be coming to meet me to say definitely whether I was North Woods Material (I had gone from a case to material), but my mother was acting on the assumption that I would be accepted.

"It's ninety-five percent definite," she said. "A Miss Springer will be visiting us."

I think that's all she said for two weeks. "Expect Miss Springer," and that was it.

I was still feeling lousy, but my mother brought the doctor back. (He was still short.) This time he gave me a vitamin B-12 shot. He said I could start on club soda, saltines and Jell-O. Later I could "move into consommé." I didn't like the sound of moving into consommé, but the B-12 shot was great. It relaxed me a little and gave me some strength, and best of all, it gave me a longing for saltines. I began craving them and that was good because I began eating something. I liked the club soda too, and my mother made me Jell-O, which I liked. I started eating and feeling a little stronger and my headache eased up a bit. I think that was partly due to the fact that I wasn't so nauseous and could keep down aspirins to camouflage the pain. Anyway, for whatever reason, it was a welcome change. After a few days I washed my hair.

This was a big time of my mother shopping, of packing open footlockers, and of the sewing on of name tapes. Everything had to have a label. Even my Kotex. (Not each one, just the box.) I remember my mother stitching away with piles of clothes, towels, blankets, laundry bags, etc., all over the living room. She wasn't speaking to me, however, just stitching away and waiting for blessed relief. The time when she would be rid of me.

I started going out every day to visit James. The first time I went out he nearly went crazy. He was across the street visiting a friend. He heard the front door slam and looked up at me and then he took off. Thank God there were no cars coming. He leaped up on me and moaned and licked my face and wagged his whole self and ran around me in circles and wouldn't stop moaning. Then he went and brought me his tug. He wanted one of our good old-fashioned wrestling matches where we play-fight, each one pulling on an end of his rubber tug with me ordering James to give it to me and him wrinkling his nose and showing his teeth and growling at me. I used to love those matches. When we had them on the front lawn people would get scared to death. People who were passing by, or something. They used to think he was really mad and think he was going to bite me. Sometimes I'd get a special wrestling hold on him and try to throw him down and he'd growl really loud and that would really drive people crazy.

Anyway, James wanted to play-tug, but I didn't have the strength. Vitamin B-12 shots and saltines go only so far. James was disappointed, but he understood. He dropped his tug and looked up at me with sad eyes and lay down and rolled over for me to scratch his belly. I love that dog.

Christmas was weird. Mother, "Miss Let's-Keep-Appearances-Up-At-All-Costs Queen," purchased a tree, small and spindly though it was, and put it in front of the window in the living room to show anyone who might pass by that everything was A-O.K. at the Beldwins'. She had my father get out the stand and the lights and colored balls and told him where they should go while he did all the work. It was sad. One of the biggest joys in my life used to be decorating the Christmas tree. Anything to do with Christmas, really. Now I didn't care. The one thing my father seemed to know how it should go (is that a sentence?) was the tinsel, which he hung strand by strand over each branch while he daydreamed of heaven knows what. I stayed in my room mostly. The whole thing was too depressing.

Penny came over with all sorts of stuff. She brought brownies that her mother had made and cookies that she had made and a Christmas puppet that her younger sister, Heather, had made especially for me. There was no act in what she did, or anyone else in her family for that matter. A lot of the neighbors put on these acts of NOT PAYING ATTENTION TO THE TERRIBLE THING THELMA DID. It was gross. I knew they were having a field day gossiping about me at their luncheons and coffee gatherings. A few like the Smiths and the Spearers seemed to ignore us, but the others made a big display. Penny's family just seemed to understand my suffering. It was beautiful.

My parents gave me no presents. I was too depressed already for that to make any difference. All that present giving just seemed dumb, like a burden to all concerned. Jennifer and Kevin gave me a nightgown. I suppose they figured that's what you do. You get a present for your sister and sister-in-law. There was probably never written in the etiquette books a section on what a newly married couple gives the sister (sister-in-law) if she has just set fire to a building a few weeks before Christmas. I can understand their confusion. The nightgown was pink and I detested it. It had a lot of lace on it that scratched like crazy and also it wasn't warm enough for Vermont. I didn't bring it up here.

Minna and Ed invited us all to spend Christmas with them in Cleveland, but thank God my mother turned them down. They sent me a traveling cosmetic case, not real handy since I don't use cosmetics, but thoughtful I suppose. I didn't bring that up here either. There isn't that much call for cosmetics in the forests of Vermont.

So Christmas was weird. I got my nightgown and my cosmetic case and my puppet from Heather, she's six. I have the puppet up here with me. It sits on the desk in my room.

We had no stocking presents which was another big difference. We had always done Christmas up in a big way. My parents got a few presents and Jennifer and Kevin stopped by in the afternoon. I went out to the garage to be with James.

One morning around eleven I heard the doorbell ring and it was Margaret Springer, the lady from NWS. She and my mother talked for a long time in the living room and then my mother brought her into my room. That little knock and then barge right in.

"This is Thelma," said my mother.

Margaret said hello and I don't think I said anything. I had just gotten into my jeans and was lying on my unmade bed trying to figure out what to do. The days stretched out before me endlessly. Nothing made sense.

"Well, I'll just leave you two alone," said my mother in her cheerful voice. "If you want me I'll be right out here."

"We'll do fine," said Margaret. (Points for her.)

My mother left and Margaret asked if she could sit down and I said "suit yourself." She sat down and started sneezing and blowing her nose. She told me she had a cold and took a thermos out of this humongous bag she had with her (I've since learned she keeps her needlepoint, her sketch pad and a tin of colored pencils in there) and poured herself a steaming hot cup of tea.

"Would you like some?" she asked. "It's mu tea. It tastes weird if you've never had it before. Would you like some?"

"No thanks." (After such a great buildup how could I refuse?)

Then she started squinting and looking around the room. She has this lousy eyesight, but she doesn't wear glasses unless she's doing some art thing, or reading, I guess, although I don't think I ever saw her read. I sat up on the bed because I felt stupid lying there, looking at the ceiling like some kind of invalid. My room was, as usual, a mess, but Margaret just sort of squinted around, not seeming to care.

"Are you going to miss this room if you go away to school?" she asked.

"No."

"Do you spend a lot of time in here?"

"Yes."

She sneezed a few times and blew her nose.

"Is that your dog I met on the way in?"

"I don't know."

"He was big and mostly black with white and tan markings. He looked a little like a collie, but not really."

"That's him."

"He's a sweet dog. I love animals," she said.

Then she told me about all the animals up at NWS and about her cat and her aunt who has this boxer and how one day he finished his dinner and then ate his dish. He must have been hungry. That same dog also ate his rubber ball. I heard that and started laughing hysterically. I mean it really wasn't *that* funny, but I couldn't stop laughing. She was laughing too, but pretty soon she stopped and asked me if I liked the idea of going away to school. I said it was all right and she said I didn't sound very enthusiastic and I said I wasn't, at which point she started sneezing again.

"Would you rather stay here?"

"No," I said.

"I hear you started a fire."

No comment.

"Why did you do that?"
(Questions! Questions!)
"I don't know."
"I've felt like doing stuff like that, but I never have."
"That's where we differ."

She asked me a lot more questions which I don't remember much of and then my mother came in asking if Margaret wanted some coffee. Margaret held up her thermos and told my mother about her mu tea. My mother didn't want any either. Pretty soon my father came tapping at my door in his gray cardigan saying he was there. He was always doing stuff like that, announcing the obvious, but leaving out the obscure. Maybe he never got that far, into the obscure. That's some distance for most people although I myself (who else?) seemed locked in the obscure with no foothold on the simple. At least that's the way I used to feel. It's a lot better now.

Anyway, there was my father in his gray cardigan tapping and saying he was there and my mother introduced him to Margaret. Pretty soon Margaret left, not, however, before making it clear that I would like NWS and she would look forward to seeing me there. I had made it. Either by hook or by crook—hook being that I wasn't a total slob and they could stand me, or crook being I was such a slob that I needed them desperately, borderline hopeless, neediest of cases. Naturally, I suspected the latter.

CHAPTER TWO

On January sixth we left for Vermont. My footlocker fit neatly in the back of the Country Squire. Jim Coales from across the way loaded it in. My father has a bad back and women don't lift things. The worst thing was saying good-bye to James. He had been aware of my leaving for several days although I never told him about it. Just one day when I was with him I realized that he knew. There was no need to tell him. I just patted him and said I'd see him again somehow, not to worry. He stayed as close as he could to me for the last few days before we left. When we were together he would always lean up against my leg. When I was in the house he would whine to be let in which he never did because he knew it was hopeless. Those last days though he just didn't care. He'd whine and whine and a lot of times if I could I would go out and be with him and take him for a walk. I pictured the two of us running away together, but I knew it would never work.

That last morning after the car was loaded up I went into

the garage. James had moaned all the time the car was being loaded and when I came into the garage he lunged at me and when I told him to get down he leaned really hard against my leg and then sat on my foot. I guess he figured if he kept sitting on my foot he could keep me from leaving. I hugged him and told him I'd see him before too long and that I just had to go. As I was telling him about it I realized that there was a tiny seed of hope deep down inside me. The tiniest seed, that maybe if I could get away from these strangers that didn't know what to do with me, maybe I could survive. Maybe I would want to. James always brought out the best in me. I gave him a big hug and a stack of Oreo cookies and left.

The ride was endless. There had been a big snowstorm a few days earlier, but it had stopped and the roads were just slushy. I was tired from not having slept for weeks and not eating or anything and I remember dozing off in the middle seat, with my parents up front and my footlocker and junk in the back. It was like a dream. I'd doze and then wake up and see the backs of my parents' heads (my father driving, of course—women don't drive when men are in the car unless the man is going to or from a hospital as a patient). My parents didn't talk to me the whole way and I of course didn't talk to them and they didn't talk to each other much. Anyway, I'd doze and keep waking up and try to keep warm by pulling coats and stuff over me, but it didn't work. My feet were freezing. My feet are always cold. I don't think my blood goes down there much.

Every once in a while I'd look out the window as we headed up the Hudson. Everything seemed so weird. Where was I going? Why was I going? Nothing made sense.

I slept for pretty much the whole trip north of the Beacon–Newburgh Bridge and didn't wake up until we hit the bumpiest road in the world. It was the road leading into North Woods School. I didn't notice the barn on the right where they keep the horses, cows, pigs and one donkey (Sachs), the wooden bridge over the creek (pronounced crick), the upper pasture, the soccer field or the vegetable gardens all along the left of the road. It's great stuff, beautiful places, but of course all I noticed then was the bumpy road.

I haven't written for so long this is giving me the creeps. I really wrote a lot in a comparatively short period of time. I mean, it's mid-May now so what I've written so far took me only two or three months. I don't remember when I started, but for the last three weeks I haven't put pen to paper, or pencil either for that matter. A lot has been going on, changes and all, which always feel weird and often put you out of commission, assuming you were in commission to start with, but these kind of changes were good, very good, but more of that later. The main trouble is I forgot how to write. I'm here at my desk with my Christmas puppet, the one made by Heather, a cross-eyed dwarf I suspect. (Not Heather, that is, the puppet.) I'm feeling like I never wrote before in my life. It's weird. Tomorrow I think I'll go back to the rec hall. Maybe that'll help.

Where was I? We were driving up to North Woods School on the bumpy dirt road and when we got up to where you park cars, we parked—or my father parked, being the driver—and my parents got out of the car. I stayed where I was in my kind of day snooze. My mother banged on the window, motioning for me to get up and come out, which I did. We wandered around, not knowing where we were supposed to go.

There's a real neat thing. Outside the main building of NWS the supporting beams, or whatever you call them, are like trees. That is, the bark is off, but the branches are partially still on, and so you can climb all over the sides of the building. My mother asked this kid who was climbing on one (the kid was Chic Rizzulo who knows all answers to all things, a good one to ask a question of, come to think of it). Well, Mother asked him where the office was and he said, "In there," pointing inside the building and then he said, "Nobody's there. You want Frank?"

"We're looking for Mr. Elder," Mother said.

"Yeah, well that's Frank," said Chic. "He's probably in his house by now. It's seven-thirty for God's sake."

My mother was none too pleased with the "for God's sake."

"Thank you," she said in her chilling way, and we went off to find Frank.

Frank and his wife, Mary, run NWS. Frank is tall and looks like a beaver, although not as fat. He's a real outdoors sort of person. He likes to climb mountains and build fences and sleep outside in sleeping bags when the weather gets below thirty. A couple of months ago we went on this mountain climb and we stayed overnight outside. The trip took two and a half days. Anyway, this really bizarre thing happened. I went to sleep in my sleeping bag, finally, after much tossing and turning and being jabbed in the stomach by pointy rocks, and woke up with frozen hair. Really. It was all frozen stiff. It was gross.

Anyway, getting back to Frank and Mary Elder, he looks like a beaver, although not as fat. So does she. She's not fat either. It must be their teeth. My feelings about them (the people, not the teeth) have changed in the months I've been here. At first I loathed them as I did everything and everyone. Then I began to suspect that they were gods. Intelligent, attractive, in good physical and mental health, busy, eating well, what more could you ask for, except maybe regularity? I'm beginning to find out. I mean it's not that they're bad, they're just closed off. Their hearts are closed. They have insulation around their instincts. They have no desire to reach for anything they haven't already experienced. If they haven't seen it then it doesn't exist. But I'm getting ahead of myself and sounding all-knowing in the process. Who died and made me boss?

ANYWAY, back then when I went with my mother and father to find Frank and Mary (or Mary and Frank) I had such a headache I could hardly walk. We followed Chic Rizzulo's instructions and found the beaver twins in a sort of small, wooden, rustic house, one of many scattered about.

I remember so little of this it's amazing! I remember my migraine and the beaverlike teeth of the Elders and not an awful lot more.

I guess we sat around there for a while and I suppose my parents and the Elders talked and I stared into space. Where we were, I later found out, was Fox House, one of ten houses at NWS. Each house has about twelve kids in it and two teachers for house parents. (Parents of houses?) Sometimes these houseparents are married (to each other) and sometimes they're not, but there's always one man and one woman and if they're not married to each other they don't sleep together or if they do they don't tell anybody.

After the talk, and my staring, Frank took us to Hollow House (the name had an ominous ring. Would it collapse? Did it matter?). Hollow House was to be my house. Betty and Bruce Crouse (married and sleeping together, at least as far as we knew) were to be my houseparents. We went in and met them and there were a lot of kids around. I wanted no part of anyone, or anything, although, as I remember, everyone was being pretty nice to me, offering me hot chocolate and popcorn.

I've come to like Bruce and Betty although Betty's obsessed with batiking, which I find weird. Bruce drinks too much beer, but they're O.K. That night I didn't notice them much, or anything else except my headache. My parents left. No good-byes, no handshakes, winks or smiles. They hate me. Well, my mother hates me, and my father being the space cadet of all time, WHO KNOWS?

CHAPTER THREE

The first week up here is a blur. I had a headache most of the time and lived on aspirins and saltines. Everything else made me throw up. All the people (well, most of them) were nice to me, but I didn't notice. My roommate was B.B. Baker. She's gone now and I have a new one (more of her later), but B.B. was the first. She was at NWS because her mother had been married and divorced eight times (I kid you not) and B.B. had a nervous breakdown. She once went for two months without eating anything but Oreo cookies (do you hear that, James?) and B.B.'s mother said the Oreo cookies caused B.B.'s mental collapse, but B.B. knew better (a good story title?). B.B.'s mother herself caused B.B.'s mental collapse of which the great Oreo cookie consumption was only a by-product, or symptom (agreed, Dr. Stone?). Anyway, the Oreo cookies, or the lack of anything besides Oreo cookies, caused malnutrition to accompany depression and B.B.'s mother took notice. B.B. had always been plump and then she turned all weak and bony.

It was a mess. B.B. was a good kid, although hard to live with. At the time we shared a room she was supposedly manic-depressive, which meant, to me anyway, that you never knew what you'd get, a wink and a smile, a joke or a stony stare. At least with me in those days you could always depend on the stare. When B.B. was in a good mood there was nobody funnier. She had this fantastic sense of humor (do I say that because it was like mine?). She would tell stories about things that happened to her or people she knew, and she'd break herself up and laugh and roll all around, all over the place. I miss her. And JAMES! HOW ARE YOU, JAMES? DO THEY FEED YOU AT LEAST? DOES ANYBODY HUG YOU, OR TALK TO YOU OR SCRATCH YOU BEHIND THE EARS. I LOVE YOU SO.

As I said before, that first week is hard for me to remember. B.B. led me around when Frank and Betty (the beavers) or Mary and Bruce weren't telling me what to do. I was really in a daze. I don't think I even thought of James, so that tells you how far gone I was. If somebody told me what to do mostly I did it. Why not? I didn't care if I lived or died, why would I care whether I went to Library or Gym? It was all one, which in a sense is true, but from the other side. (Is that clear?) I did anything "they" (meaning everyone except me) wanted. I did it all unless it took too much energy.

This is a good time to describe this place. It's in the woods (which you may have gathered from the name, although I wouldn't try to gather anything from Maplewood, New Jersey, name or otherwise). But North Woods School is in the woods—dependable of it to live up to its reputation—and it's really beautiful with mountains all around. It's green any time of the year because of the pine trees (not found on Pinetree Road).

There are about 120 kids with a big "teacher-kid ratio," which means there are a lot of teachers. At first I was discouraged to learn this, but actually the teachers here are fairly decent. I'd rate them on an average of 7 on a scale of 1 to 10, although there are exceptions. There's a minus 1 in the kitchen—Bertha. She weighs upwards of 250 pounds and I strongly suspect her of sweating into the food (which is generally gross enough without her sweating into it). Anyway, Bertha is mean and German (am I prejudiced?) and wears large black hairpins which any day I expect to find in my vegetable soup. Bertha always yells at you when you clear. (We rotate this as one of our many jobs.) Nobody ever clears fast enough or stacks right and Bertha is always screaming about it. I understand that Bertha's meanness, not to mention her sweating, has been brought up at many government meetings and Betty and Frank always talk about how she's under a lot of pressure cooking for so many people and we have to be understanding and everything. I expect, however, that the day Betty finds a hairpin in her creamed chicken she'll sing a different tune. (If indeed she sings at all.) Lately we've taken to calling Bertha "Mean Bertha," and that seems to have taken the pressure off the kids, if not off Bertha.

Well, so, Bertha's a minus 1 and Larry's at least a 12 (more about him soon). It just occurs to me that I hate it when other people rate things and people on a scale of 1 to 10. It sounds so arrogant and bitchy. Why did I do that? Is it because I'm arrogant and bitchy? I hope not. It also occurs to me that Bertha isn't technically a teacher so none of this makes any sense.

There are also a lot of doctors and psychiatrists and psychologists and stuff here who I wouldn't presume to rate because who gets to know them? We're all divided into houses (except the doctors who live somewhere else) with the kids all mixed up. (In more ways than one.) What I mean is the sexes and ages are mixed. (Sexes—male and female; ages—twelve through eighteen, plus the kids of the teachers—any age.) It's supposed to be more like a family that way. As I said before, each house has two houseparents, one man, one woman.

There's a real looseness up here and I gather that not every "juvenile offender" is suited to it. They don't even force you to do homework but they try to make it interesting (motivation) and basically it works. They're after a community feeling, which is beautiful, and a responsibility for your own actions, which is a bitch. It's really getting down to basics. They trust you here which was so weird at first, but it seems to work. They trust you and you find yourself living up to that trust. Well, a lot of kids do, of course, not all. Some commit suicide and others they send away.

I remember on my first morning here I had intentions of staying in bed.

"You can't do that," said B.B. She was sitting on the edge of her bed, lacing up her Red Wing work boots.

"What do you mean?" I said, half awake, my head throbbing beneath my covers.

"You can't stay in bed. Gotta get up. Gotta move."

"Who says?"

"They do," said B.B. She got up and stamped her feet, letting her jeans fall down over the tops of her boots. "You have to go to everything—classes, doctors, sports, meals, chores, you name it. You either go or they send you to the infirmary."

"I'll go to the infirmary," I said.

"I wouldn't."

"Why not?"

"It's a bummer." B.B. began putting on sweaters. I've never seen anyone put on so many sweaters. Five, I think, or seven, or ten.

"I just want to sleep," I said.

"Good luck."

"What do you mean?"

"Mary Lorraine."

"Who's that?"

"The nurse. She's a nonstop talker. And boring! Forget it!"

"I'll sleep."

"She'll wake you up. She has this needlepoint she does and she goes into a trance. She just stitches away and talks. She doesn't care what she says or how many times she says it. I kid you not. I was in for strep throat last month and nearly lost my mind. She sat around for hours doing this needlepoint of fungus growth and a tree. It was gross." B.B. finished putting on her sweaters and sat on the edge of my bed. Her outer sweater was dark blue. She looked like a giant blueberry. "She's crazy," said B.B. "She sat for hours stitching this hideous mushroom and talking about hurricanes in Florida and how they cause floods and how they have to put sandbags down, but they don't serve any purpose and how it's a shame. I kept pretending to be asleep. She didn't care. She just kept on talking. You better get up."

I pulled off my covers and tried to stand. The room was freezing and began to spin. My head felt like it was about to explode.

"I'll wait for you," said B.B.

"Thanks," I said. "Why do you wear all those sweaters?"

"It's cold."

"Why don't you wear a jacket?"

"I like variety."

B.B. waited while I dressed and we made our freezing way to the dining room. We always eat in the main building except for Sunday-night supper which we have in our houses. It's about a five-minute walk to the main building from Hollow House.

"Cold up here, isn't it?" said B.B. She had put on a muffler and pulled it up over her nose.

"Yeah," I said.

I'll die of frostbite. I'll never see the dining room.

"I hope they have pancakes," said B.B.

"Don't talk about food."

"Why not?"

"I'll throw up."

As I said earlier, I remember very little of my first week at NWS. I kind of walked through everything in a daze with my headache and not really caring if I lived or died. For chores the first week I had to help Frank (of the beavers) repair a fence out behind the kitchen. I did what he told me to do, I think—I guess I must have—holding poles, pounding with mallets, and then it was over.

That first week also (of course) I met Dr. Stone. (Are you with me?) Ever since I've been here I have to go to him three days a week for fifty minutes each. The first time as

I remember, he TALKED but not since. HARDLY A WORD! I don't think I saw the office that first time. I hardly saw him. Glasses. I remember his round glasses and that was all.

"What do you think of this place?" he asked.

"I don't know."

"Do you like it so far?"

"It's all right."

"Have any questions?"

"No."

"When did you arrive?"

"I don't remember."

"Day before yesterday, wasn't it?"

"I don't remember."

"Have you been away from home before?"

"No."

"Do you miss it?"

"No."

"Where's your home?"

"New Jersey."

"In the suburbs?"

"Yes."

"Have you lived anywhere else?"

"No."

'How about your family? Any brothers or sisters?"

"A sister."

"Younger?"

"Older."

"What's her name?"

"Jennifer."

"Do you get along?"

"No."

"Does she still live at home?"
"No."
"She's at college?"
"No."
"Married?"
"Yes."
"What do you think of her husband?"
"He's a jerk."
"What makes you say that?"
"Who knows."
"Something about him puts you off."
"Yeah."
"Tell me about school. You went to public school?"
"Yeah."
"How did you like it?"
"It stank."
"What didn't you like about it?"
"Everything."
"Do you have any thoughts about this place yet?"
"No."
"Any questions?"
"No."
"I'll be happy to answer any questions you have."
Silence.
"Thelma, you'll be coming here for sessions three times a week. It's your time. You express what thoughts come into your mind and that way I can help you. We can get at the root of your discomfort."
Silence.
"You'll only hurt yourself by withholding your feelings here."
Silence.

"Are you having any thoughts now?"
"Can you give me something for my headache?"
"You have a headache?"
Isn't that what I said?
"Yeah."
"Have you tried aspirin?"
"Yeah."
"It doesn't help?"
"No."
"Is it a very bad headache?"
"Yeah."
"How long have you had it?"
"A couple of months."
"Have you had a checkup?"
"Yeah."
"What did the doctor say?"
"He said I was fine."
"Is anything else bothering you? Sore throats? Weakness of any kind?"
"I get dizzy and nauseous and sometimes I can't sleep."
"You have trouble sleeping?"
Isn't that what I said?
"Yeah."
"I'll give you a couple of tranquilizers. Have you taken tranquilizers before?"
"No."
He reached into his drawer and took out a flat cardboard package with two pills enclosed in cellophane.
"You can take one tonight and one tomorrow if you need it."
He gave me the trancs and I took one as soon as I got

back to Hollow House. It helped. I could still feel the headache, but I didn't care. I felt kind of floaty and way back somewhere was this headache, but it just didn't get to me. I could feel the pain and everything, but I felt oddly detached from it. I don't like trancs anymore although they seemed to help in my earlier days here. Now meditating is better. I get pretty much the same things from it, well, the good things, but none of the rest. I feel relaxed and free from anxiety, but not vague the way I used to feel on trancs. They were fun at the time though. Now I've lost my taste for them. Things are better this way, so why go back? But I'm getting ahead of myself.

CHAPTER FOUR

It's funny the stuff that brings you back. I keep saying that the first week up here was all a blur and I remember the moment that changed. Outside my window is this bird feeder. It's the kind for only very tiny birds, with a sort of rodlike ledge, or bar (that's the word) across the front connected to this metal strip, and if a too heavy bird or anything sits on it, the feeder closes. Well, I woke up this particular morning and there was this humongous squirrel upside down on the bird feeder, hugging the feeder and sort of gripping the top of it with this back paws. He was all sort of wrapped around the feeder, sucking out the birdseed. I saw that and started laughing, like I couldn't stop. B.B. came in from the bathroom. "Look," I said, pointing to the squirrel. She started laughing and we were both laughing. I think the squirrel stopped being funny to us after a while, but it was one of those things where the sound of our laughter broke us up. You know those times. It's like they can go on forever.

That was a Sunday and Sunday mornings are spent mostly

in our houses unless there's some trip with Frank or something up some mountain. That morning when I came back from breakfast with B.B., Chic Rizzulo had on the record of Christopher Plummer in *Cyrano* and he (Chic, that is) was jumping all around on the furniture and everything with this sword. I think his father had given him the sword before he disappeared. Nobody seemed to know where Chic's father went, or if they knew they weren't telling Chic. Chic had the secret opinion that his father had joined the Foreign Legion but I doubt it. I bet he's in jail somewhere or running a hotel in Las Vegas. Anyway, there was Chic, leaping and lunging all over the place, mouthing the words to *Cyrano* with the record blasting away. When we came in he lunged at us and said something like, "Forsooth, young maidens that you should be untimely ripped." (Isn't that Shakespeare?) "Perchance some evil doth prevail."

"Cool it," said B.B. "Nobody wants you leaping around."

(You could tell what kind of mood she was in.)

"Methinks she doth protest too much." (Definitely Shakespeare.)

"Don't get rowdy," said B.B.

"Ah ha! What evil lurks beneath the heart that beateth not for me?"

"I wouldn't know," said B.B., and she started for the stairs to the bedrooms. Chic leaped in front of her and blocked her way.

"Not so fast, fair damsel."

"What a wally," said B.B. "You're a royal pain."

"Referest thou to me?"

"Damn right," said B.B., and she gave Chic this big shove (B.B. was strong) and he lost his balance and fell back against the wall and B.B. stormed up the stairs saying, "Time for murder, time for murder." She didn't like Chic.

I kind of like Chic. He's always coming at you from behind corners with these weird schemes. Not sexual, I mean like trading things, or making bets, or playing stupid tricks on people. He makes me think of this character in this book *Catch-22* called Milo Minderbinder. He had schemes like Chic. I loved that book, although the movie pretty much stank. It did, however, have my favorite actor in it, Alan Arkin. He played Yossarian, the central character, and he was terrific as usual and especially HANDSOME in that movie. I like his looks anyway, but I think he looked best of all in that movie. He's been my favorite actor for several years. Some kids prefer obvious dummies, actors who can't act which is one of the things I feel it's important to do if you're an actor. Good actors (and actresses!) can pretend to be different people, which after all is what it's all about. (Do I want to be an actress? I sound so passionate all of a sudden. Maybe it's just Alan Arkin who brings that out in me!! I thought I wanted to be a writer.) Anyway, his characters are all so different. It's hard to believe one man could play them all. I think the real thing about Alan Arkin is he knows something. I can't describe what I mean. Maybe he's a Yogi.

Well, getting back to Chic. After B.B. pushed him against the wall he turned off the *Cyrano de Bergerac* music and sat down on the couch.

"I'm sure she did that," he said.

"Did what?"

"Knocked me against the wall," he said.

I didn't want to go up to the room and be with B.B. in

her present condition so I sat down on the couch. It was quiet now at least, without the *Cyrano de Bergerac*.

"She's hard to figure," said Chic.

Just then a whole bunch of kids came back from breakfast. Renny and Steve, Pigway (not his given name) and Muffin. Muffin is adorable. She's the eight-year-old daughter of Betty and Bruce. She's a real tomboy, but kind of small with straight blond hair. I like her a lot, partly, I suppose, because she reminds me of me at that age. (Are you with me, Dr. Stone?) Last week there was this big to-do up here because Muffin got mad about something and disappeared. They found her in the town wandering around. She had tied all her stuffed animals to herself. She had fifty-one, I think. Fifty-one stuffed animals all tied on with rope and string and sashes from bathrobes and a couple of belts. What a sight she must have been.

Well, I was sitting with Chic when Muffin came in with Pigway and these other bigger kids and although we had just had breakfast Pigway made straight for the fridge. Pigway is humongous. I think he's fifteen and he eats all the time and talks with his mouth full. He's starved for affection, but he'll never get it if he doesn't stop chewing with his mouth open. He is gross. Well, Pigway took all this food out of the fridge. We're allowed to keep snacks in there, but only food which is good for you. Pigway detests it, but eats it anyway. So he got all these organic snacks and started to eat. Muffin sat on the floor to play jacks. I used to play jacks when I was younger but I forgot all about it until I saw her playing. She's good. Well, Muffin was playing jacks, Pigway was stuffing his face and Renny was moving all over the place trying to decide what to do. She never sits still. Thank God she's not my roommate. I'd much prefer B.B. with all her ups and downs. Steve is this kind of mean black (brown?) kid who is always putting people down. He sat down next to Chic.

"What's he doing?" asked Steve, pointing over at Pigway.

"Scoffage," said Chic. "He's munched out."

"Can't blame him," said Steve. "He hasn't eaten in ten minutes."

"Poor guy," said Chic. "It's pathetic."

"Leave me alone," said Pigway, and he got up with his organic snacks and went upstairs.

I heard a weird thing about Pigway's mother. I heard that she sleeps all day and is up all night and (here's the weird part) she's a painter. What does she do for light? What do painters need? North light? South light? Whatever it is, Pigway's mother doesn't get it. I also heard that she locks all her paintings in the closet and won't let anybody see them.

After Pigway went upstairs my housemother, Betty, came in with Muffin's little brother, Michael. She sat down next to me on the couch. She was out of breath from running all the way from the main building. After she sat down and caught her breath she mentioned just having seen Bimbo. Bimbo is this terrier up here who belongs to one of the math teachers and she has this thing where she has to jump off the roof. (Not the math teacher, the dog.) There's this tin roof over the dining room in the main building and at the back there's a hill like, and it almost touches the roof. Over the front side it's a very far way down to the ground which was where Bimbo did her jumping. Really. Like every day, several times a day, you'd pass by and this dog would go sailing through the air, right in front of you. It was weird. We all used to laugh about it, but last week on one of her jumps Bimbo broke her leg. It was so sad. Her leg is in a cast now and she sits around staring up at the roof a lot. The thing that scares me is I know the minute the cast comes off she'll start jumping again and I'm really worried about her getting hurt. She's a nice dog. Maybe we could put up a fence.

Anyway, Betty sat down next to me on the couch. She's helped me, but she's into batiking in a way that puts me off. It shouldn't. I should get past that, but it's hard. Whenever someone tries to help me, or give advice, or anything, I always wonder if I take their advice will I turn out like them. I think that's wrong, really. I think it's good to be able to learn from everyone, but you have to be careful. Betty needs to batik. It's like her security blanket, and I find that weird. But she has helped me to know myself a little better and that's a good thing.

After Betty caught her breath and told us about seeing poor Bimbo staring up at the roof with her cast on, she asked us what our plans were for today. About then I realized that I didn't have a headache. My headache was gone. (I sound like a T.V. commercial, but it's the truth.) My headache was gone and I had forgotten to take my trancs that morning. Progress. I had been up here seven days (check this, T.B.) and although tuned out for practically the entire time, here was a glimmer of progress. One thing I know that helped. It was great not seeing my parents (or my sister!). It really was great and I do not feel guilty about that. I mean it's now almost May as I write this. I have not seen them for over three months and I don't miss them one bit. It's awful living with strangers who you're SUPPOSED TO LOVE and you don't even like them or know who they are or anything. It's such a relief up here. I'm not SUPPOSED to be close to anybody up here, so any feelings of liking, or loving, or caring are gravy. The pressure's off and that's a blessing!

Everybody has to write to their parents (or at least to one parent) once a week on Sunday nights which is a good thing, really. I mean you do it because you have to and then it's over and you don't feel guilty (hi, Dr. Stone) for not having written. Also you don't feel stupid for having written to people you don't care about because it wasn't your idea in the first place. It all works out pretty well. That first Sunday I just wrote:

Dear Mom and Dad,
I am here and alive. Please, take care of James.
Thelma

I couldn't bring myself to write "Love, Thelma." Thank God it wasn't required.

CHAPTER FIVE

As I moved into my second week up here, my sessions with Dr. Stone (yes, you!) became torture. As I said, the first week he mainly asked me questions and gave me trancs, but the second week he STOPPED TALKING. It was horrendous.

This time I noticed the office. It's kind of plain with two chairs (comfortable), a desk and a narrow couch, some bookcases, a couple of pictures on the wall (one picture of some European town—French?—in the rain and a map of Long Island). There are pamphlets around and a ceramic duck on his desk and that's about it except for the owl in the bookcase. I sit in one of the chairs and this wooden owl stares at me from the bookcase. (It's not enough you have to stare at me, Dr. Stone, I also need the wooden owl.)

Well, the first session of my second week I went in and sat down as I had done the week before and there was this SILENCE. I have never known such silence. I mean it was different from the silence in meditation. There it's peaceful and still and deep. This silence was screaming and aching, furious, a special kind of torture out of which good things come no doubt, but it's NOT FUN.

For a while I just sat and stared at the owl, thinking, I'll just sit here until he tells me to go. What's so hard about that? But I found out. After about fifteen minutes (I'm guessing on that. It seemed longer, but I don't think it was) I felt this enormous urge to run screaming from the office. It was hell to sit in the chair. I felt that old gnawing pain in the small of my back and I wanted to stand on my head, or scream, or smash everything in the office. I'd start with the owl and end with Dr. Stone! I tried to hold on and lasted about another five minutes. Why should I talk? I thought. That's what he wants. He told me that last week when I wasn't listening, but I remembered. I'll never talk. Let him give up on me.

Finally I began to feel faint. My headache had returned. I had shortness of breath. I felt I couldn't get enough air and my heart was pounding. That stupid owl was staring at me from the bookcase and so were you, Dr. Stone, behind your oval glasses.

"What's this supposed to be, anyway?" I blurted out. "What are we doing just sitting here? What's the point of this?"

"What would you like to do?"

"Leave," I said.

"This is your time."

"It stinks."

"You feel it stinks."

"It stinks."

"Why?"

"What's the point of this, just sitting here?"

"Is there something you'd like to talk about?"

"No."

More silence. Again, the heart pounding, trouble breathing, dizziness, fantasies of smashing things.

"That owl is ugly."

"What do you find ugly about it?"

"Everything. You have rotten taste. If you mess with my brains will I have taste like you? I'd rather die."

More silence.

"When can I leave?"

"This is your time."

(Say that again and I'll smash your face in.)

"What's 'my time' about it? You force me to come here, tell me to sit down in this chair and then you stare at me and don't say anything on top of which you have rotten taste and I'm forced to study this stupid and hideous owl not to mention your disgusting duck."

"The duck on my desk?"

"I cannot believe I am spending my time this way. Is this what you do for a living?"

"What bothers you about my duck?"

(The best question I have ever heard.)

"It's a useless piece of hideous garbage."

SILENCE.

"Can I leave?"

"This is your time."

(He said it! All right, now, make good on your threat. Punch his face in.) But I couldn't. I started to cry.

Silence. Just me crying.

"What's mine about it?"

"About what?"

"What's mine about this time?"

"As I told you last week, you come here three times a week for your sessions. During this time you're free to express your thoughts. Anything that comes to mind. This way we can get at the root of your anxieties, relieve the difficulty, make you more comfortable with yourself. I can't analyze you if you don't talk."

SILENCE.

I stared at the owl and began counting to one thousand by fives. My breathing got heavier. I began getting nauseous. I was about to throw up on his oriental rug when FINALLY he said—real calm and casual, almost cheerful—"Well, that's all the time we have for today." As if we'd done something!! Maybe we had. I mean, I know my work with him has helped me, but it was sure hard to see it that day.

He got up and started for the door and opened it and I got up and left. I remember walking very slowly down the long corridor, hoping not to vomit all over everything. There were these shelves along the walls with pottery and ceramics and stuff that the kids had made. It was pretty ugly stuff, but all of it was better than the owl, or the duck. I can't get over how Dr. Stone could have paid good money for them. Maybe somebody gave them to him as a gift, but he must have thought they were all right, otherwise why would he have them in his office and look at them every day? I'm so upset about his taste! Why does that matter? Things that matter, things that don't.

Down at the end of the hall was a whole section of Betty's batiks. (Two *B* words.) I stopped there and took a lot of deep breaths. There was a water fountain there and I leaned on it. Chic popped out from around the corner.

"Whatcha doin'?"

I didn't answer. Basically I was afraid that I'd throw up.

"Hey, are you O.K.?"

"I don't know. I feel sick."

"You want me to walk you back to the house?"

"Ya."

People can be nice sometimes.

CHAPTER SIX

Larry says I don't remember the first time we met. I've mentioned him before and said it was too early to talk about him, but now's the time. Larry is the Phys. Ed. teacher up here and also my yoga teacher. He makes no big deal about the yoga, outwardly, that is. Inwardly is another story. But I mean he's not cultish, or weird at all. He doesn't wear an unusual costume and also he doesn't talk about yoga much. Only if you ask him a question he'll answer, that's all. He's this terrific person who you can trust—that's mainly it—and he lives what he believes. A new world opening up to me, but I'm getting ahead of myself.

Larry is about thirty-five, slim with dark eyes and a great smile. He's married to this nice lady, Ellen, who teaches English and they live at NWS. They're houseparents at Wood House. I sure would like to be there, but that's kind of unfair to Betty and Bruce who are really decent. Anyway. (This seems to be getting rambly. There's so much to say about him, but I can't say it all at once.)

Larry says we met in the library during my first few days up here, but I have no memory of it. The first time I remember seeing him was in the gym. I was taken there by B.B. because we were both scheduled for volleyball. (Get that ball over that net!) I remember seeing Larry at a distance. I'll never forget. He looked at me and smiled his great and knowing smile (what did he know?) and held up a hand. No wave, just a steady hand. What's he so happy about? I thought. He must be dumb or a retard or something. I could tell the smile was genuine. It couldn't be that he was faking it. I just ignored him, or tried to, and sat down in the corner of the gym. Everybody else started playing volleyball and Larry paid no attention to me as I sat, staring into space.

After a while, he came over and sat down next to me and the AMAZING THING was that he didn't ask me why I didn't want to play volleyball. He didn't even mention volleyball. That caught my interest. Then the REALLY AMAZING THING happened. He was sitting there, saying nothing and watching the kids run around and punch the ball. I was wondering why anybody would want to do that. The only sport I liked was riding. I thought of this place out in New Jersey where I used to ride when I was maybe ten, or so. It was a great place, but then the owner's wife died and the man sold the horses and moved away. SO LARRY SAYS, "When the weather turns warmer we'll be horseback riding."

It was like my stomach turned over. I had no question about coincidence or anything. I knew he knew what was on my mind and I also knew that he knew me better than anyone else had ever known me. Even better than I knew myself. Strange, but true. Although it didn't feel strange. It was just nice. It was like coming home. I couldn't help smiling which was unlike me in those days. We didn't talk anymore that day. He had to help referee the stupid volleyball game and then he took some kids on a camp-out somewhere, so I didn't see him again for several days. Dunce that I was, I forgot all about him.

Pretty soon after that was the first time I saw Snapper. I was on my way from Art to my house when right in front of me walked this HUMONGOUS THING that looked like a beast of the jungle. It was Margaret Springer's cat, Snapper. Snapper is reported to be a regular cat, but I'm not convinced. He's the size of a large bulldog (believe it or not), so when I first saw him I got scared. Like I thought he might attack me and bite me in the neck the same way a vicious rabbit did in this Monty Python movie. But Snapper just came over and rubbed against my legs, almost knocking me over, and then he flopped down on my feet (ouch!). I was patting him when Margaret Springer poked her head out of the window of Pine House and said, "Hello."

"Hello," I said.

"Would you bring him in for me?" she asked. "I have to leave soon and I don't want him out."

"It's a good thing he's friendly," I said. Then I bent down and picked up the heaviest animal I can ever remember lifting.

"He's a sweetie," said Margaret. She left the window and went around to open the door for me.

I went in and put Snapper down on the rug. Nobody else was there.

"Hello, you big gorgeous thing," said Margaret. (She wasn't talking to me.)

She bent down and scratched Snapper behind the ears. He

rolled over and fell to the floor with a thud.

"He's the most gigantic thing I've ever seen," I said. "What is he?"

"He's a cat," said Margaret, scratching Snapper along his belly. "How ya doing, you big old cute thing? You are so special."

Snapper began to purr the loudest purr I have ever heard. Margaret was kneeling down scratching his belly.

"He's my friend," she said. "Aren't you, Snapper?"

"Where'd you get him?"

"He belonged to a friend of my cousin's. She didn't want to keep him when he started getting so big because she has a small apartment. You like that, don't you?" she said to Snapper, scratching and scratching his furry belly. "He was a regular-sized little kitten, believe it or not. Weren't you?"

"That's hard to believe."

"I know."

Looking at Snapper is so weird. It's like some bizarre sequence in a horror film. My feeling is that the friend of Margaret Springer's cousin was terrified of Snapper the way I was on our first meeting and didn't want to admit it so she blamed everything on the size of her apartment. People go to such lengths.

"You want some cider and a cookie?" asked Margaret.

"Sure," I said. Who am I to turn down a cookie (right, James?).

We went into the kitchen and Snapper followed us and jumped up into the sink and sat there, sucking the water out of the tap. (He should meet that squirrel from the week before.)

"He always does that," said Margaret. "I leave the water

just barely dripping and that's the way he drinks. He won't drink from a saucer."

It was weird. We had our cider and cookies, oatmeal raisin—not chocolate, but good—and Margaret asked me about how I was getting along and all. I told her "all right." I didn't really want to talk about it. Then she said she'd like to have me stay longer, but she had to leave for meditation group.

"You want to come?" she asked.

"No thanks."

I remembered a notice about the group meeting a couple of times a week on the bulletin board (that sounds like the group met on the bulletin board, but I'm sure you know that's not what I mean), but I wasn't interested. I figured there was enough to do that I had to do, without doing stuff that I didn't have to do.

"You can stay here with Snapper and the cookies if you want," she said.

"I think I'll leave," I said.

"O.K.," she said.

"Have you been meditating long?"

I remember being surprised to find myself asking her the question.

"About two years," she said.

"I've tried it a few times," I said. "What does it do?"

"It's a bridge to my soul."

Now that struck me as the most pretentious thing I'd ever heard. I understand now what she meant. I've experienced that sensation, but then, it really put me off.

"It's the center of my world now," she said. "I started getting intrigued with what was true. Truth started to interest me. Now it's a passion."

"Nobody cares for truth in New Jersey."

"Oh, some do," said Margaret. "You have to know how to look."

"I think my parents are allergic to it."

"To truth?"

"Yeah."

"Give them time."

"They don't need time. They need major surgery."

"You sure you don't want to stay here with Snapper? He'd love the company."

"No thanks," I said.

When we left, Snapper was still in the sink, sucking on the water tap.

CHAPTER SEVEN

The next day I had a relapse. Not that I was so far along to start with, but wherever I was I went backwards from there. I staggered through my classes in a dazed depression and after lunch I went back to my room. We were supposed to be out playing ball, or glazing pots, or doing something constructive, but I wasn't up to it. I went back to my room. B.B. was out somewhere planning a cookout, so I had the room to myself. I lay down to take a nap and thought of James. My darling James. I pictured him pulling on his tug, running to meet me at the school bus, drooling over his cookies, licking my face, backing into my legs, chasing sticks. The more I thought about him the more lonesome I got. I started to cry. JAMES! I MISS YOU JAMES! MY ONLY FRIEND IN THE WORLD AND I DESERTED YOU. DO YOU UNDERSTAND? DO YOU FORGIVE ME? ARE YOU REFUSING TO EAT? STARVING YOURSELF IN LONELINESS AND CONFUSION? DO YOU SPEND YOUR DAYS AND

NIGHTS LOOKING FOR ME? WAITING FOR A GAME OF TUG? I WANT TO KISS YOUR NOSE.

I remember I got up to close the window which some imbecile had left open for some incredibly stupid or at the least obscure reason. It was ten below zero! Why open a window? I had been freezing there on the bed for at least a half hour, but I was too miserable to care until my teeth started to chatter and I started shaking.

"Stupid idiot," I mumbled through my tears.

I slammed the window shut. Then a really terrible thing happened. I get the shivers thinking about it. I was seized with the feeling that James was dead. It was so awful. In my mind I could see him lying on the garage floor. He had been there for days. No one knew. Maybe they knew. They didn't care. They would put off dealing with a dead dog. It's not tidy. Then they would have to. It would be untidy to leave him. (Tidiness motivation.) Anyway, untidy to leave a dead dog in the garage, so call the man (always a man) to come and take the body away. NO!!!!! NOT MY JAMES!!!!!

I got a chill. I sat on the edge of my bed. Everything was still. No motion, deathly calm. Only my heart pounding in my chest. James was dead. I knew it. He had died of loneliness. He had stopped eating. My parents were keeping it from me "for my own good." Don't upset Thelma any more than she already is. In time we can tell her. When she gains the strength to deal with it. It's for her own good.

"NO!!!!" I screamed. I fell down on my knees on the cold wooden floor and put my head on my bed and sobbed.

Betty came in, cheeks rosy. Jogging in the snow?

"What's wrong, Thelma?"

"Nothing."

"You're upset. What's wrong?"

"Nothing." I stopped crying. I didn't want to talk.

"You sure you don't want to talk about it?"

"No."

"Maybe I can help."

"No."

"Maybe I can."

"When I want help, I'll ask for it."

"All right. I can't force you."

She left. I put the pillow over my head.

Maybe I'll stop breathing. I want to die too.

I thought of my trancs. Dr. Stone had given me a couple of trancs at our last session. I had asked for a bottle but he just gave me two. I guess he thought I might overdose. I got up and took one and sat on the edge of my bed. I took several deep breaths. Then I thought of writing to Penny. Remember Penny of Pinetree Road? (Another title?) Equally happy vacuuming or going to the movies? I'll write her, I thought. I'll ask her to check on James and tell me if he's dead. I tore a page out of my notebook and wrote this. I was still crying.

Dear Penny,

I'm very worried about James. My parents hate him and I guess they feed him, but that's about all. Would you go over and check on him and write and tell me if he's O.K.? It's very important. My address is North Woods School, Lake Bomoseen, Vermont. Thank you.

Thelma

I finished the letter and then got an envelope and a stamp from Betty and took it to the office for them to mail it. After that I went back to my room and fell asleep.

In the morning I had a session with Dr. Stone. (Yes, you.) I hadn't planned on confiding in him, but he was there and he was listening and I was so upset about James.

"Good morning," he said, greeting me at the door. He was so cheerful behind his glasses. He looked right at me. How could he be so cheerful? Couldn't he see my tiny red eyes, all puffed up from crying through the night? Couldn't he see me wavering as I walked to my chair, the room shifting before my eyes? He just closed the door and walked briskly to his chair and sat down. His sport jacket was so neat, his slacks so pressed, his shirt so clean, everything in order. (How does he do it?) He smiled and then just stared at me. I looked down at the rug and started to cry. I felt about three years old.

"Are you having any thoughts?" he asked.

"My dog is dead."

"Your dog died?"

"Yes."

"I'm sorry to hear that. Did you get a letter from home?"

"No."

"They phoned?"

"No."

"How did you find out?"

"I just know."

"What makes you think he's dead?"

"They hate him. They keep him in the garage and they just feed him and that's all. They never talk to him or anything. We were so close. I know he's dead."

"Don't you think they would have let you know?"

"No."

"Why not?" He was still cheerful, optimistic. I was in pieces, sobbing, my nose running all over my hand.

Why doesn't he offer me a Kleenex? Doesn't he have them? He never cries.

"Why wouldn't they have let you know?"

"They wouldn't want to upset me. They probably think if they told me I'd burn down the school."

"Why would they think that?"

"I burned down Ethical Culture."

"You burned down Ethical Culture?"

"Well, I didn't burn it down, but I set fire to it. Nothing happened, which was the worst part of the whole thing. You must know about that. It's the reason I'm here."

"Would you like to tell me about it?"

"No."

Silence. More tears.

"Why not call your parents and ask them about your dog?"

"They'd lie. They wouldn't tell me. I don't want to talk to them anyway."

"Would you like me to call and ask them about it?"

That's nice of him. That's thoughtful

"They wouldn't tell you. They don't trust psychiatrists. Well, my mother doesn't and my father's out to lunch."

Silence.

"What's your dog's name?"

"James."

"What kind of dog is he?"

"He's part collie and part something else. His mother was a collie."

"Sounds like a nice dog."

Silence. Tears.

"Well, that's all the time we have for today."

What? Still cheerful? Sending me away, untended, with the only friend I have in the world lying dead in a garage in New Jersey?

Dr. Stone rose and headed for the door.

"If you change your mind and want me to give your parents a call, let me know."

"I won't change my mind."

I left the office and went down the hall and into the bathroom where I shut myself in one of the stalls for a couple of hours and cried.

CHAPTER EIGHT

Two weeks went by and I still hadn't heard from Penny. My obsession with James' death was coming in waves. Every time the terror started I'd take a tranquilizer and that would take the edge off it, but it kept coming back. Some days I would worry that James was dead, some days I would know it and some days I would just miss him like crazy. Some days I guess I didn't think about him at all, but that was rare. I often wondered why Penny didn't answer my letter. I don't know why I didn't think of calling her. Dr. Stone had taken it upon himself (as they say) to call my parents and inquire after James' health. He told me that my mother said James was fine, but of course I didn't believe her.

One day around then, Chic convinced me to come with him to meditate. He used to meditate in his room sometimes and he asked me to join him, but I didn't. The first time he asked me to go with him to the meditation group I didn't either, but then he asked me again and I figured, why not? It seemed pretty dumb, but not as dumb as a lot of the other stuff the kids were doing like punching volleyballs around and remembering the dates of things. I had tried meditating at "home" as I mentioned, but it didn't "work." I never knew what was supposed to happen, but I did know that whatever it was, it wasn't happening, or if it was happening, I wasn't aware of it. A few moments of peace was all I remembered and I didn't rate that very high. A few moments of peace! That's a fantastic thing! An incredible beginning! I hadn't had a few moments of peace since I could remember. Maybe never.

The second time Chic asked me to go with him to the meditation group I went. The group meets in one of the English rooms a couple of afternoons a week. They push the tables and desks to one side and put pillows down. Everybody takes off their shoes. It's nice. I went in with Chic and there were lots of kids there, maybe twenty or so, and Margaret was there and Sarah, one of the history teachers, and Bill, the Russian teacher and, surprise of surprises, there was Larry. He smiled his smile, with raised hand once more, and I found myself smiling back. I suddenly felt very nervous, like I felt in kindergarten just before going on as a carrot in the class play. I took off my shoes and sat down with the others. After a few moments Larry began to lead the meditation.

"We come together in peace, we come together in harmony, we come together in love. . . ."

That sounds good.

I remember having the feeling that I was beginning something important. With my mind, it made little sense. Gathering with these people. Sitting together in silence. Dumb. A waste of time? But underneath where it mattered, I felt I had begun. We sat together in silence for about twenty minutes. The first fifteen of those minutes seemed like an eternity. My back hurt, my legs hurt, my nose itched. I felt funny about moving because it didn't seem like anyone else was moving and I didn't want to ruin the meditation. (How odd of me to be concerned with what other people were doing. Strange. Out of character.) Finally I had to scratch my nose. It truly felt like a matter of life and death so I had no choice. I scratched it and nobody seemed to mind. Maybe they didn't know. I was on the point of giving up on the whole business when something in me shifted. It was as if I was inside out, now just outside my skin, on the outer edge, instead of being locked inside. I felt very tall, an enormous distance between my head and my legs. Everything in me relaxed. Before my mind flashed a pyramid in Egypt, familiar. On top of it was an eye, like on our American dollar. What's this? I thought. My heartbeat accelerated. I felt excited.

"Peace," said Larry.

Our meditation was over. The pyramid stayed in my mind. I didn't want to leave. I heard people beginning to move, shift their positions, but nobody said anything. I began to wonder if all the others had their eyes open. Would I look silly with my eyes still closed while everybody else's eyes were open? I opened my eyes. People were sitting around, some smiling, others staring, their minds elsewhere. Nobody talked for about ten minutes. Sarah, the history teacher, got up and went over to her shoes. She began to put them on.

"That was nice," said Margaret. She put on her glasses which she had taken off for the meditation.

"Yeah," said Chic.

Several of the kids smiled. Then they got up and started

putting on their shoes. I just sat there.

"How do you feel, Thelma?" asked Larry.

"Fine," I said.

That's an odd answer for me. Do I really feel fine? How rare.

"I remember the first meditation I had with my teacher," said Larry. "I was sure I had blown the whole thing. I didn't know what I was supposed to be feeling, but I was sure that whatever it was, I wasn't feeling it."

"I felt like that when I meditated with my friend Janice," I said.

"I know."

What did he mean by that?

Larry continued. "I remember my teacher asked me how I felt. 'O.K.,' I said. 'Are you happy?' he asked. 'Yes.' 'Did you hurt anybody?' 'No.' 'Then you did good.' "

I guessed I must have done good too, at least for the last five minutes.

I didn't meditate by myself after that first time, which surprises me. I remember how I didn't want to come out of that first meditation, but even with that I stayed away from it for almost a week. I don't even remember thinking about it much. Of course that was the week Peter Westmiller arrived so that might have had something to do with it. Peter is this incredibly adorable assistant history teacher who came up in February. He's Sarah's assistant this year, but next year, because of his incredible charm (number one), brilliance and brains (numbers two and three), will have classes of his own. Several of the girls fell in love with him on first sight, me included. Maybe some of the boys fell in love with him too, but they'd never tell, at least they'd never tell me. Anyway, he is ADORABLE. (If he ever reads this I'll die.) He's twenty-three, with brown hair and light brown eyes that crinkle at the sides when he smiles. He wears kaki (sp?) pants and button-down shirts and V-necked sweaters and sneakers. He's warm and sweet and seems entirely oblivious to the havoc he's wreaking. (Is that what you do with havoc? Wreak it? I think you do.)

The first time I saw him was in History. I came in late and he was just there. Just like a regular person, as if he wasn't handsome and adorable and sexy, just regular. When I say handsome I don't want to give the wrong impression. He is handsome, but not Mr. Pepsodent, if you know what I mean. Offbeat, something like Alan Arkin. Simple with a complex overlay, rough, but gentle. Cute. Anyway, there was Peter when I came in late to History.

"Hi," he said, and my legs felt instantly like Junket. "Come on in, I'm Peter Westmiller. Sarah had to go to a meeting so I'm taking the class today. I'll be her assistant for the rest of the term."

Forever, please! Don't leave at the end of the term.

"What's your name?"

"Thelma," I said in a tiny voice. I collapsed at my place at the table, dropping *American History* and *Algebra* loudly on the floor.

"We were just discussing the Boston Tea Party."

Why didn't I wash my hair?!? It's been almost two weeks. Oily stringy hair. I wish he couldn't see me. I love his eyes.

The class was a blur—heart pounding, body like Junket, no sense whatever of tea, not to mention Boston. After class I ran all the way back to my house and washed my hair.

Maybe he won't recognize me, I thought as I stood in the

shower, sudsing up. Let him not connect the two people. At dinner he'll see me with clean hair and he won't know I'm the same disgusting person from the Boston Tea Party. He won't know how ugly I can look.

After my shampoo I put on my pale green crew neck sweater that I kind of like the way I look in and waited for dinner. He wasn't at my table that night. He has been since, though, and at such times I never know what I've eaten. This first night he was way on the other side of the dining room, so I found myself planning the strategic move of getting to the exit door at the same time he did.

"Hi there," he said.

"Hi." Forced, casual delivery on my part. Playing it cool.

"Do you find the Boston Tea Party boring?"

"NOOO!!!"

Why am I shouting?

"That's good."

Oh, God, he remembers me. He recalls my grossness. Pre-shampoo and green sweater.

"When you didn't say anything I figured you were bored. I had a lot of boring teachers in high school and I vowed never to bore a student. It's not so easy."

"Yeah. I can imagine."

"Well, good night."

"See ya."

Peter Westmiller put spice in my life. I waited eagerly for History, washed my hair every day, wore my green sweater a lot and looked around corners for the sight of him, but otherwise there was still me. My panics, my headaches, my pig eyes, my loneliness. I was always there, waking and in dreams. That part was a bummer.

CHAPTER NINE

When Chic reminded me about the next meditation group I told him I didn't want to go. I was tired.

"Come on," he said, "come on," and he wouldn't let up. He just kept saying "come on." It was so weird. He just stood there saying "come on" over and over again. I think he would have said "come on" for hours, days maybe, I don't know. Anyway, finally I said I'd go. It seemed easier than sitting in my room listening to him say "come on" all afternoon. I guess that's what he figured.

After all that, the meditation seemed meaningless. I was waiting to shift out of my skin and see pyramids with eyes, but it didn't happen. It was kind of relaxing for the first ten minutes, but after that I just wanted it to be over.

"You mustn't judge your meditations," said Larry, as I sat thinking I had definitely blown it this time. A failure once more as with everything else in my life.

"Do you remember what I told you?"

"About you and your teacher?"

"That's right."

Pause.

"What did I say?"

"You said he said, 'Are you happy?' and you said, 'Yes,' and he said, 'Did you hurt anybody?' and you said, 'No' and he said, 'Then you did good.' "

"What else did I say?"

"That you thought you had failed?"

"That's right."

"Yeah. I wondered why you told me about that. I wasn't feeling like a failure at that moment."

"I know."

Pause.

"Now do you see why I told you?"

"To prepare me?"

"That's right. When you know these things you have a responsibility to enjoy yourself."

That went by me. What did he mean? I let it pass.

"The mind isn't up to the task of evaluating a meditation. It's something else altogether. Continue your meditations faithfully, not too long at a time—five or ten minutes for now—whatever is comfortable. Find a comfortable position in a place where you can be by yourself, place your mind in your heart and leave yourself alone."

B.B. thought I was crazy. I meditated only three times that week, but two of those times she walked in on me. The first time I was sitting cross-legged on my bed with the closet light on. (Larry says it's good to have a little light in the room when you meditate so that's the way I work it.) I thought B.B. would be at chorus until nine, but she came back early in one of her moods.

"What the hell are you doing?" she asked.

I was really mad at her for interrupting me, because an extraordinary thing was happening. As I have mentioned so many times I have this gross sinus condition which causes pig eyes and headaches and what was happening was that my sinuses had suddenly started to drain. I had been meditating for about five minutes when suddenly it was like Niagara Falls. Blessed relief as they say in the Dristan commercials. (Husband: "Honey, I don't know how you do it. And you with a virus cold." Wife [nasal; carrying a turkey]: "Oh, I feel much better now." Video: drawing of inside of a puffed nose as it shrinks. Then the announcer says something about Dristan shrinking swollen membranes fast, for blessed relief.) Anyway, there I was, no Dristan, nothing, just peace and quiet and Niagara Falls. My headache went instantly away and then B.B. came in and yelled at me.

"What the hell are you doing?"

"That's not very nice," I said. "For God's sake, that's no way to come into a room." I turned on the desk lamp.

"What were you doing, sitting there like a zombie, for God's sake. What was that?"

"Never mind."

"No, tell me."

"Forget it."

"Don't act weird around me. I hate that. Tell me what you were doing."

"I was meditating."

"Meditating, for God's sake. That is weird."

"You're the one who's weird."

"What's that supposed to mean?"

"Here today, gone tomorrow."

"What do you mean by that?"

"Forget it."

"Get out of my sight," said B.B., so I went into the bathroom to meditate.

It surprises me that I started meditating at all. Meditation is such a big deal these days it would be like me to keep my distance. I hate anything everybody is doing. Points off. Like if I go into a store to buy something, which I rarely do, but when I do, if the saleslady says "It's what they're wearing," right away I don't want it. Unless it's blue jeans. Blue jeans and yoga, the only "in" things in my life. Yoga is truly a big deal these days, and in that way it tends to be sickening. Higher consciousness T-shirts, sweaters, greeting cards, iron-ons, posters, teas, you name it. This girl up here, Tuffy Trackenburg (she arrived two weeks ago. Her mother had her seventeenth affair in two years and Tuffy locked herself in the basement and wouldn't come out), anyway, Tuffy told me she went to the restaurant in Los Angeles where they have Nirvana eggplant, Shakti enchiladas, samadhi salad, and ananda fruit punch. Stuff like that verges on the ridiculous. There's such a fad aspect to the whole thing and that tends to negate its value. But there's something there. Already I can tell and I've been meditating, what? three months or so? (An enlightened soul at my Smith-Corona.) Maybe the main thing that endears me to meditation is the dwindling of my headaches. Truly, the draining and the dwindling have been divine. But I hope it's more than that.

I don't know if this is going to work. I have my writing places which are my room and the rec room, and I always have the stuff with me that I'm working on, the stuff I just finished. That way I have something to refer to, which I hardly ever do, but at least I have it handy. I'm now in Margaret Springer's kitchen. It's warm and cozy and quiet here, too quiet. In the rec room there's always kids screaming and records. The noise helps. It's always pretty noisy at Hollow House, and the surroundings are familiar. Here it's quiet and unfamiliar and I don't have my notes or anything, so I feel kind of naked. (What do you make of that, Dr. Stone?) Be that as it may (all things considered), here I am, alone, in Margaret Springer's kitchen. I don't know where all the kids are. I was supposed to meet Margaret here to help make posters for the horse show. Assumably my love of horses will make up for my lack of painting talent. We shall see. Margaret's late because she had to take Snapper to the vet. He probably has ear mites (Snapper that is, not the vet) because he's been shaking his head and staring at the wall all week. That's what cats usually do when they have ear mites. Anyway, here I sit, waiting for Margaret and Snapper, sipping some mu tea which Margaret left in a thermos for me. It's not bad. I saw this pad of paper and a pencil lying on the table (put there on purpose by Margaret? Thank you). I'll give it the old college try, or should I say reform school try? Where was I? Oh, yes, meditation.

"I've been meditating," I said by way of challenge to Dr. Stone. (Hi, there.) He sat behind his glasses, in front of his owl, to the right of his duck, waiting for me to say something else.

"I've been meditating. Don't you care?"

"Would you like to tell me about it?"

"Not if you're not interested."

"It's important for you to express whatever thoughts come into your mind."

Why is he being so cold? He hates the idea of meditating. He thinks it's stupid, worthless, dangerous. What do I care what he thinks?

"I've been meditating with Larry's meditation group. Do you know about it?"

"I've heard something about it."

"What do you have against it?"

"What makes you think I have something against it?"

"It's obvious."

"What are your feelings about it?"

"It's only been a few weeks."

"Do you like it?"

"I guess so."

"You sound unsure."

What is he doing? Undermining the one thing I've found to give me a moment's peace? How dare he?

"It's only been a few weeks."

"You said that."

Punch-in-the-face time.

"It relaxes me. My sinuses drain. Sometimes my headaches go away."

"That's wonderful."

Good for you, Dr. Stone.

"What's your opinion of it?" I asked.

"I have an open mind about it. I've heard it can be very helpful in some cases. Perhaps you can tell me more about it. I'd be interested."

Points for you, Dr. Stone. You could learn from me. That's a nice admission.

"You're finding it relaxing and helpful with your sinus discomfort. Seems to me you should keep it up."

O.K.

CHAPTER TEN

A couple of weeks after Dr. Stone gave me the green light to meditate, a decidedly gross thing began to happen. I was meditating a little more often, being careful to stay out of B.B.'s way, and getting into it in the sense that I would look forward to it. That was good, but then this terrible thing started happening. I'd sit there and let my mind sink into my heart and it would be nice for a minute or two. The endless tape would quiet in my head, blessed relief, my sinuses would begin to drain (sorry for verging on the disgusting here once more), my headache would ease and then it would happen. My mind would go to James and I'd see him, dead, in the garage. It was awful. I couldn't stand it, so every time it happened I'd stop meditating. The image would fade after a while, but I was definitely left with the creeps. I'd be upset and scared for days after. The whole thing was disgusting. I couldn't meditate and that scared me. I had found this corner of peace for the first time in my life and now that was invaded by horror. Where was there a place for me?

After it happened a few times I went to talk with Larry. I found him out by the gym, mending a volleyball with great care and attention. He's like that. He always pays great attention to detail, even with seemingly stupid things. He was mending a volleyball and it was like open-heart surgery. Not tense, but thorough.

"Hello, there," he said.

"Hello." I sat down on a large, freezing rock and leaned my back up against the side of the gym.

"Do you think we can save this ball?" he asked.

"I don't know."

"I don't either. Look at this. The stitching's completely out on this side."

"You can't restitch something like that, can you?"

"I don't think you can, no. What do you think of tape?"

"What kind of tape?"

"Ah. That's the question. What kind of tape?"

"Masking tape wouldn't hold."

"I don't think so."

"It wouldn't last through a game."

"We need something stronger."

"Do you have anything stronger?"

"I have this." He picked up a wide roll of silver tape and held it up. "It's a very strong tape that's used mainly on movie sets. Edward gave it to me." (Edward is Pigway's given name. Pigway's father produces movies.)

"That might do it."

"It might. The surface of the ball has to be very clean, though, otherwise it won't adhere properly."

"I see what you mean."

Are we going to talk about volleyballs all morning?

"What's up?"

"What?"

"What's the trouble?"

"Oh . . . I can't meditate."

"Why not?" He continued his operation on the volleyball. He was rethreading the frayed stitching as best he could before applying the tape.

"I see my dog." (Tears.)

"Yes."

"I have this wonderful dog, James, and every time I start to meditate I see him, dead, in the garage."

Larry stopped work on the volleyball and looked at me.

"I was worried about this all last month and then it got better. Now it's all right except every time I start to meditate it comes back."

"What do you do when this image comes into your mind?"

"What do you mean?"

"You begin your meditation, the image of your dog comes into your mind and what do you do?"

"I stop meditating." (Tears.) "It's horrible. I can't do anything else."

"All right, wait a minute now."

I was crying so hard I was shaking. Larry put his arm around me. "Hold on now." He reached into his pocket and took out a folded wad of Kleenex. (What I kept wanting you to do, Dr. Stone. How about the arm around the shoulder? Probably that too.)

"Here," said Larry.

He always seems to have Kleenex in his pocket, but I've never seen him use it. I've seen him offer it to other people a lot, though. I bet that's why he carries it.

"Let me tell you something," he said. "There's a power that rises up from inside of you, from inside all of us, and this power is stronger than your illusion. Don't hide from this thing, this dark, unfounded fear, this illusion that your dog is dead. Don't put up a wall. That very effort will give the fear its strength. Let it in. Let the fear into your meditation."

"I can't."

"Yes, you can. Let your illusion be bathed in the light of this power already within you."

It sounded like a fairy tale. I wanted something real.

"I don't see how it can work. Even if I had the guts to go back and meditate and see it again, which I don't . . ."

"You do."

"I don't. It's like hitting myself over the head."

"It's the opposite."

"It is?"

"Sure it is."

"I don't understand."

"Just do it."

"I don't see how it can work."

"Just do it."

"All right."

It sounded crazy, but I figured I had nothing to lose. Another bout with the terrors, but I'd been through them before.

"Good," said Larry. "Now would you hand me that tape? Let's see what we can do for this ball."

That evening B.B. had a bread-baking workshop, so after supper I came back to the room, turned on the old closet light, took my position on the bed and began. Drain, drain. Niagara Falls. Blessed relief. PEACE. James. James. JAMES! DEAD! DEAD ON THE COLD GARAGE FLOOR. CEMENT. GARBAGE CANS. ALL ALONE. DEAD. NOOOOO!!!!! RUN TO HIM! SHAKE HIM! MAKE THE DEAD GO AWAY! I HAVE TO STOP! I CAN'T STAND THIS! JAMES!!! DON'T STOP. DON'T HIDE. DON'T RUN. OPEN. LET THE FEAR IN. OPEN YOUR HEART. STAY WITH IT. LARRY. LARRY. JAMES!!! IT HURTS. TEARS. SOBS. HOLD ON. I LOVE YOU, JAMES! I LOVE YOU! —And then—an enormous wave of peace.

I'll never forget it. My dear, dead James, dissolved in a bath of light. The fear, shrinking, spinning off, farther and farther away. Light. Silence. Peace.

After several minutes I opened my eyes and sat, motionless on my bed. My arms and legs felt heavy. It was like I was wrapped in electric fluff, cotton candy without the stickiness, everything soft. I stayed there just like that for a while. I don't remember how long. Ten minutes? An hour? Then I got up and put on my pajamas, turned off the closet light, got into bed and slept for fourteen hours.

CHAPTER ELEVEN

"You're not going to like this."

"What's that?" said Dr. Stone. He was puffing on a pipe for some reason. I didn't remember seeing him do that before.

"You know my panics about James' being dead?"

"Yes."

"They're gone."

"That's wonderful."

"Wait till I tell you the whole story. I got rid of them by meditating."

No response. I knew he wasn't going to like it.

"You don't believe it, but it's true."

Silence.

"Why aren't you saying anything?" I asked.

"What would you like me to say?"

"Whatever you feel."

I sound like you, Dr. Stone.

Silence.

I decided to go on or we'd be in for forty-five minutes of silence. I could see the handwriting on the wall, not to mention the map of Long Island.

"I knew you wouldn't believe me. This thing started happening where whenever I started to meditate the fear would come and I'd see James, dead, in the garage."

"Go on."

"Well, I got scared to meditate. I told Larry about it and he said to let myself picture it. That there was a power inside me that was stronger than my illusion. He said to allow the fear to come into my meditation and it would be washed away. I tried it and it's gone."

"That's wonderful."

"You don't believe it."

"Do you?"

"I know it's gone. I can tell that."

Pause.

"I guess I'm afraid it will come back."

"Why?"

"How could something like that work? It's too simple."

"Why do you expect the fear of your dog being dead to return?"

Why does he have to state the whole fear like that? Is he testing to see if it's really gone? Is it? I don't feel anything.

"Why not accept your new level of comfort? Don't you feel worthy of that?"

"What do you mean?"

"Events have transpired in such a way as to relieve your anxiety. You could enjoy that, but instead you insist upon dwelling on the possibility that your good fortune will disappear. I'm suggesting that perhaps you don't feel worthy of feeling good."

"Could be." (That sounded snide.) "I shouldn't think you'd believe in meditation. I mean if meditating relieves anxiety, what does that do for the analytic process?"

"Nothing that I can see."

"What do you mean?"

"I wouldn't look a gift horse in the mouth."

Is he reducing meditation to a gift horse? I've always liked horses. Gifts too for that matter.

"Different people respond in different ways," he continued. "Seems to me your meditating is beneficial."

Seems that way to me too.

I just read Plato's "The Cave" for English and I may never be the same. I don't know what made me begin the assignment. I mean I'm still not doing all that much schoolwork. More than I used to, but that's not saying an entirely great deal. I was intrigued by the sketch our teacher gave us that went with it. I think I wanted to find out what the sketch meant so to do that I began "The Cave."

It's all about this thing Plato asks you to picture which is really like life and what people do to themselves and the struggles to break loose and everything. To me the cave was Maplewood, New Jersey, but I suppose it's like most places on this earth. I have to talk to Larry about this. I feel it's so closely related to what he talks about. I couldn't find him tonight so I'll sit here and write about it, which I guess is the best thing for now.

In "The Cave" Plato asks you to picture this cave where there are these prisoners. The prisoners have been there since they were children (not babies, which I find interesting). They are seated, chained to the wall, and they can't turn their heads because of the way they are chained. It's dark in the cave, but there's a tunnel out to the daylight. Behind these prisoners and above them is a gigantic fire and between them and the fire is a road and a sort of curtain. People walk along the road. Some carry things, some talk, and because of the big fire behind them they cast their shadows on the opposite wall, the one the prisoners stare at. The prisoners are bent and stiff and uncomfortable and all they see are these shadows on the wall which they take to be real (not just shadows, that is). Then Plato says to picture one of these prisoners being asked to get up and climb up the big hill toward the blinding fire. It would be PAINFUL! His (or her) muscles would ache from not having been used and having been cramped up for all those years. Then because of being in the dark so long the light of the fire would almost be blinding and that would hurt. If she (or he) were asked to look at the real people walking down the road the prisoner wouldn't be able to see because he'd be blinded by the light. He'd (or she'd) think you were crazy for insisting there was anything there. O.K., so assume this prisoner makes the climb and slowly his or her eyes adjust to the light and he or she starts seeing and breathing and standing up straight and getting to know the stars and the sun and the moon and the planets and everything. Then this person would start to feel sorry for the others back down in the cave sitting in the dark all twisted up and bent and everything, staring at a bunch of stupid shadows on the wall. So he or she might go back down into the cave and try to let them know that there's a whole universe outside and there's no need to sit all twisted up and bent in the dark, staring at a bunch of shadows. But the prisoners in the cave think he or she is crazy when he or she comes back down. First of all he or she has been in the light so long that he or she can't see in the dark anymore and he or she kind of stumbles around, bumping into walls and everything and worse than that he or she has LOST THE KNACK OF ANALYZING THE SHADOWS! He or she can't even see the shadows anymore. "What?" say the prisoners. "That person wants to take us on a journey? For what? To where? There can't be anywhere else. I've never seen it. That's proof. Anyway that person can't even function right. Stumbling all over the place. Can't speak the language. What kind of a leader is that?" So if this person who was outside the cave came back to help the others they'd probably try to kill him or her because they'd think he or she was either crazy or mean. (Jesus and Joan of Arc come to mind and Socrates too for that matter.)

That is such an amazing thing to me. Really. It's like the cave is Maplewood and part of the creeps I was getting is that I knew there was something else outside and nobody else I knew knew that because they had never seen it. But deep down they knew and that's what made them grouchy. My parents and everyone else that used to drive me up the wall. They mainly suffer from limited visibility.

I have to talk to Larry. I had been suspicious of Plato's *Republic* when I first saw it listed on my English assignment. More crap was my feeling, but was I ever wrong! They sounded like such great guys, Socrates and Plato. I wish I could have known them.

CHAPTER TWELVE

April and May went so fast. Peter Westmiller was getting more adorable daily for one thing. Basically, he didn't pay any attention to me, but there was the famous marshmallow roast. We were having a campfire one night, the whole school, with singing and marshmallows and everything. It was nice, but then it turned into sheer brilliance. What happened was I was sitting there with my little stack of marshmallows and my stick, all bundled up in my red-and-black-checked lumber jacket with my muffler and my gloves and my wool cap. I was between B.B. and Tuffy Tracktenburg and there was this space between me and Tuffy and who should come over but Peter W.

"Hi, cutie, mind if I sit here?"

Well, I tell you, that carried me through several weeks.

"NO!"

Don't shout. Speak like a human person.

He sat down with his marshmallow stick and his twinkling smile.

"Can I share your marshmallows?"

Anything. Take my life.

"Sure."

"How many have you got?"

"What?"

"How many marshmallows?"

"OH!"

Don't shout. Keep calm. "One, two, three, four, five, six, seven."

"Have you ever tried to divide a marshmallow?"

"No."

"It doesn't work."

"Here. Take four."

"No. Two's enough."

"Take four."

"Just two."

"Here's three."

"Thank you." He stuck a marshmallow on his stick and began toasting.

"I love these things," he said.

"Me too."

"They're best when they're crispy."

"I know."

"Crispy, but not burned."

"Oh, no."

"They can be almost burned."

"But not quite."

"If they're burned they get dry and flaky."

"I hate that."

"They're better toasted than plain though."

"I know what you mean. I don't even like them if they're not toasted."

"I don't either."

The talk wasn't too personal, but WHO CARED? HE WAS SITTING NEXT TO ME AND CALLED ME CUTE! After our marshmallow seminar there was group singing. What a night!

For weeks after that before I went to sleep every night I reran the whole scene from "Hi, cutie," right through "This Land is Your Land," the last song.

Another thing about April and May was the riding. I was at the barn every day and still am as I write this. B.B. loves horses about as much as I do, so every morning we'd get up at 6:15 A.M. (who me?) and put on our stuff for barn chores. You only have to do barn chores for two weeks a season, but we don't care. We brush and curry, feed and water, walk and exercise the horses and clean the stalls too. Every afternoon we have rides.

There are nine horses and one donkey, Sachs, but my favorite is Pete. (Is there something about that name?) Pete is a beautiful roan gelding, small, fast, but smooth. He's loving and sweet, but he won't let you touch his nose. (Tuffy Tracktenburg won't let you touch her nose either. She ran into somebody and broke her nose on their head in Los Angeles. Now she can't stand anybody to touch her nose. She says it doesn't hurt, or anything, it just gives her the creeps.) Anyway, you can't touch Pete on the nose so I'm working with him on it. I think someone must have hit him in the nose once, poor thing. I'm trying to get him used to being touched on the nose by giving him carrots, and while he's eating I gently stroke his nose. He tolerates it now, but he still doesn't like it.

There was one special ride that I remember. There were six of us—me, Larry, Tuffy Tracktenburg, Chic, Pigway and

Muffin. B.B. was supposed to come too, but nobody knew where she was. I was riding up at the front with Larry as I usually like to do. Well, I always like to do it, but often the other kids muscle in and sometimes Larry is on a horse that doesn't get along with Pete. Ringo is like that. He always puts his ears back and sometimes kicks out when I bring Pete up close. When Larry's on a horse like that he sends me back to bring up the rear. He likes to have a strong rider at the rear to keep an eye on things and I must admit that I'm one of the best riders. Muffin is a good rider too, but she's only eight and that's kind of young for the responsibility of watching the others. B.B. usually brings up the rear when I don't, but as I said, this day she wasn't there. I thought Larry would send me back, but instead he sent Tuffy Tracktenburg. She rides pretty well and is very responsible. Just before Larry sent her back we were heading out in a group across the meadow and Tuffy all of a sudden started telling us this bizarre story about her great-aunt.

"My great-aunt is such a character," said Tuffy.

I wondered what made her think of her great-aunt just then. Who knows?

"What did she do?" asked Larry.

"Well, she's always after a bargain," said Tuffy. "I mean, she lives for bargains."

"Wait up," shouted Pigway. He had fallen behind as usual. He stinks as a rider, but he always wants to ride anyway. Horses seem to resent his weight, or maybe it's his attitude. This day he was on Strawberry Danish, a well-meaning but slow horse, who at the moment had decided to turn around and stare at the barn. Pigway was kicking him like crazy, but he didn't really want the horse to move because he was afraid of falling off. Strawberry Danish knew this and figured, why not have a look at the barn?

"Let's go, Edward," said Larry. "You're holding everyone up."

"It's this stupid horse," said Pigway.

"He's smarter than you think," said Larry. "You don't mean business. Pull on your left rein as you kick."

Pigway pulled on his left rein and kicked, and Strawberry Danish moved out for Larry's sake and the sake of the rest of us. Tuffy continued her story.

"Well, my great-aunt loves a bargain."

"Mine too," said Chic. He was riding Mexi-pep, a small gray horse who never walks, always trots—the bumpiest gait in the world. A horse like that drives me up the wall, but Chic seems to like her. He sits there, bouncing away and smiling, his muffler trailing in the breeze. He has a cute way of wearing his muffler.

"Would you let a person get a word out?" said Tuffy.

"No problem," said Chic.

"Well, my great-aunt loves a bargain."

"You said that," said Chic.

"And she's in the Safeway shopping, right?"

"Right," said Chic.

"O.K. So she's getting all this stuff, shopping away, and she sees the pumpkin seasoning on sale for half-price, so she buys it, right?"

"She loves a bargain."

"Right. So she buys the pumpkin seasoning, but the incredible thing is that she doesn't have a pumpkin and the even more incredible thing is that she doesn't like pumpkins."

"I don't either," said Chic.

"Would you mind?"

"No problem."

"O.K., so not only does she not have or like a pumpkin, but nobody else in her small but entire family has or likes a pumpkin. There's just my great-uncle, Mel, and he hates pumpkins."

"I wouldn't go that far."

"Would you mind?"

"No problem."

"So what does my great-aunt do?"

"She buys a pumpkin."

"You want to tell the story?"

"Go ahead."

"O.K., so she buys a pumpkin and makes this disgusting pie that's hard, like rubber, she never baked a pie before, and nobody will touch it, never mind eat it, so she puts it in the freezer until this lady comes over for dinner that she hates and she unfreezes the pie and she's all ready to serve it, but the lady arrives with a Bavarian mousse."

"Mooo!"

"Would you mind?"

"No problem."

"What did she do with the pie?" asked Larry. He was laughing by this time. So was I, it was so silly, mainly silly of Tuffy to be going into the whole business.

"She threw it out."

"She threw out the pie?" Larry found it hard to believe. "What did she do that for?"

"I don't know," said Tuffy. "It was so unlike her."

"Strange are the ways of the world," said Chic.

About then we were at the edge of the woods where you pick up the dirt road. Larry sent Tuffy back to bring up the rear and I stayed up next to Larry. We rode in silence for a while. For some reason I was thinking about James. I guess it was the pie which reminded me of Penny (remember she baked me a lemon meringue pie?), which reminded me that I hadn't heard from her. Could something really have happened and she didn't want to break the news to me?

"Your dog is fine," said Larry.

He was doing it again, like the first day I met him, in the gym, like after my second meditation. He knew what I was thinking. Again it felt like my stomach turned upside down.

"Why am I worried again? I thought I was over that."

"You are. It's just a memory of how you used to feel."

"It doesn't feel like a memory."

"I know, but that's what it is."

We were quiet for a while.

"Your friend may not have gotten your letter," said Larry. "Why not write her again?"

"O.K."

Just then I saw B.B. She was way up ahead by the side of the road, sitting under a tree. I could tell something was wrong. I had the impulse to go to her which was so unlike me. I hadn't been noticing what was going on with other people, or if I did it didn't get to me. I had my own suffering to do.

"Can I see what's wrong?" I asked.

"Go to her. We'll rest here."

CHAPTER THIRTEEN

I rode up and stopped by the tree. B.B. sat completely still, staring straight ahead. She wasn't wearing her jacket, just her jeans and a "Property of the N.Y. Knicks" T-shirt. It was cold out.

Why isn't she wearing a jacket? She never plans to leave this tree. What makes me think that?

"We thought you were coming riding."

No answer.

"You feel all right?"

B.B. didn't move, or answer, or anything, and I got this creepy feeling. I got off Pete and led him up nearer to where she was sitting. On the other side of her, slightly behind the tree, I saw her blue ski jacket and laid out on top of it very neatly was her army canteen, a large bottle of Excedrin and two smaller bottles of pills.

Suicide.

A shiver ran through my body.

"What's that for?"

"Get the hell out of here," said B.B. She kept staring straight ahead.

"What are you doing?"

"Beat it."

"What's the setup?"

"I'm warning you."

She still wasn't looking at me. I led Pete over to a nearby tree and tied him up. I wanted him out of the confusion. I could sense what was coming and so could he. He turned to watch me as I moved back to B.B. He mistrusted the whole scene.

"Why don't you put your coat on? It's under forty."

"I don't need a God damn weather report—I need to be LEFT ALONE!"

"What's the setup?"

"It's not hors d'oeuvres."

"I got that."

"I swear to God if you don't get out of here, I'll kill you."

Now, normally, that would put me off. Not because I valued my own life all that much, but just because the whole business would have seemed like too much trouble. I'd lose interest. But this day was different. I just found myself with B.B. and not leaving. I moved around her and squatted down by her jacket and all the pills. The two smaller bottles were labeled tranquilizers and some kind of antihistamine tablets, stolen probably from Sally Marlene, or Mary Lorraine or whatever her names are. The bottles were still full, as yet unopened.

"What's the setup?"

B.B. whipped her head around, looking at me for the first time, eyes on fire.

"You touch that stuff and I'll knock your teeth down your throat."

"Quite an assortment. Mix and match."

"If you're not out of here by the count of ten, I'll smash your face in."

There was a large rock at her side. She reached out for it with her right hand.

"I swear to God, I don't care anymore. I'll do anything. You better get out of here."

I knew she meant it. I was scared, but I couldn't leave.

"Come on, B.B."

"One."

"Please."

"Two."

"B.B."

"Three."

"Talk to me. Tell me what's wrong."

"Your face."

"What?"

"Your face in front of mine."

"B.B., please."

"Get the hell out of here."

"B.B."

"Four."

"What happened?"

B.B. began laughing.

"What's funny?"

"You know it's against the law to kill yourself? How about that? They arrest you for committing suicide. Not for attempting. Attempting is O.K. No arrest. They only arrest you if you die. I find that highly practical."

"This isn't funny."

"YOU MIGHT AS WELL LAUGH AS CRY!"

"B.B." I was getting uncomfortable in my squatting position, and slowly sat down. My legs had gone to sleep.

"IT'S MY RIGHT TO SAY WHETHER I LIVE OR DIE!"

"What happened, B.B.?"

"What difference does it make? Something always happens and I'm SICK OF IT! NOW, GET OUT OF MY SIGHT AND LET ME DO ONE THING MY WAY!!"

For some reason I thought of B.B.'s horse, Butterscotch. B.B. doesn't really own her, but it's like she does. She takes complete care of her and feeds her and rides her every day. I know in Butterscotch's mind B.B. owns her. In B.B.'s mind too.

"Butterscotch didn't understand why you didn't come today. She looked confused when we left her at the barn."

"You stink, you know that?"

"Why?"

"YOU STINK!"

"What did I do?"

"You're trying to break me down. Messing with my brains. I HATE YOU!"

Then B.B. began weeping and shaking.

"She loves you. You take care of her and you're good to her and she loves you."

"GO AWAY!!!!!"

"What happened?"

"I CAN'T STAND IT ANYMORE!" She was shouting as if she wanted somebody who was far away to hear her. "I CAN'T!! I CAN'T!!"

"You can't what?"

"EVERYBODY CRAPS ON ME! IT'S ALL THE TIME AND I CAN'T STAND IT!"

"What happened?"

B.B. began crying softly now. She put her head down and wept. After a while I asked her again.

"What happened?"

"It's stupid. It's not even what it is. It's just that and everything else. I hate myself and nobody else cares about me. I don't see the point."

"What?"

"I got a letter from my mother. We were all going on a trip to Mexico this summer. The whole month of August. The school was going to let me go. I mean it's stupid. I was just looking forward to it and then she writes that it's not a good time. I AM SO TIRED OF BEING CRAPPED ON!! I COULD KILL HER!!! It's not a good time for *her* is what she means. It's a great time for me, but not for her, so it's not a good time."

"Why can't she go?"

"She and my stepfather, Daniel, split up. She's been married eight times and every time she breaks up it's more of a mess. This time she ran off with this guy who's twenty-two. I know him, he's a creep, he's stoned out half the time and she's forty-five. She left my sister and my little half brother all alone and they didn't know where she was so Daniel kidnapped them and ran away to Canada. SO IT'S NOT A GOOD TIME! IT'S NEVER A GOOD TIME TO DO SOMETHING FOR ME!"

"You call this an answer?" I pointed to the pills on her jacket.

"I just want to stop hurting. That's my right."

"You want to kill yourself and end things, but you don't end things that way. You just put them off."

"I don't want any of your reincarnation crap. If that's what you're into I don't buy it."

I don't know where this next part came from. One thing I know I was talking as much to myself as to B.B. This was stuff I'd been going over a million times in my own brain, but it was jumbled. B.B. forced me to make it clear.

"Will you listen to me?" I found myself saying. "There's a thing I know. People crap on each other all the time and sometimes people are good to each other, but the main thing is you crap on yourself. You gotta come to that. You do it to yourself. You gotta come to that finally and quit blaming everybody. They don't do it to crap on you mostly, anyway. Mostly, they're not even thinking about you. Hard to take, but true. They're just trying to do the best they can and it just isn't very good. You're the one who craps on yourself. You decided that you're supposed to go—that it's the best thing. But maybe it's not. Maybe you would have gone and gotten diarrhea the whole time, or sunstroke, or the plane might have fallen down from the sky. Maybe you'll be in love with some gorgeous NWSer by then and not want to leave. Who knows? Maybe it's a great thing you're not going on this trip. How do you know? I mean everything's the same basically. Today's the same. Everything's the same except you're not going to Mexico. The weather's the same, you've got the same friends, the same T-shirt. We'll have the same turkey dinner we would have had if you were going to Mexico. Butterscotch waits for you just the same for the afternoon ride. You're the one who's lousing everything up with your thoughts. 'My mother doesn't love me. If she did she'd take me to Mexico.' That's bullshit. She loves you. She loves you the best she can. She just can't do any better. She's trying to get along. That's the best she can do. She loves you as much as she can love anybody."

"Hold me. Hold on to me."

B.B. reached out her arms, but not in my direction. She was completely disoriented. I put my arms around her and we both cried.

"Why do they have us?"

"Different reasons. We can make it, B.B. See, I know that. I know we've got to try."

We stayed that way for a long time, crying together. After a while I wiped my nose on my shirt sleeve.

"You got any Kleenex?" I asked.

"No."

I reached over and picked up the Excedrin bottle. It had one of those special safety caps that are so hard to open. I fussed with it and finally opened it and took out the cotton on the top and handed it to B.B. for her nose.

"Use this."

"Thanks."

"Do you ever have those feelings where things seem beautiful, perfect? Moments? Like when you're galloping really fast across a wide meadow, or swimming in the ocean, or camping out under the stars or singing a really great song with a group of kids and it's like life is passing through you? You don't have to do it, it's just happening. You feel connected and everything makes sense."

"I guess so."

"You must have had that riding sometimes."

"Yeah."

"Do you get the feeling when it's over that you're coming

back to your senses?"

"Yeah."

"Back to reality."

"Hard, cold life."

"What if it's the opposite?"

"What do you mean?"

"What if those special moments are when you've come to your senses and all the rest is a distortion?"

"Crap on your sense."

"Right."

"I don't know."

"I think it's true."

B.B. blew her nose into the cotton.

"Want to go see Butterscotch?"

"What time is it? It must be too late to take her out."

"Probably, but you could give her a carrot."

"Yeah."

"What do you want to do with this stuff?"

"I don't know."

"I could just give it back to Sally Mary. Say I found it somewhere."

"Mary Lucille."

"Lucy Lorraine."

"Annie Lorrie."

"Let's go."

I picked up the pills and stuck them into my pockets. Then I helped B.B. into her jacket.

"Come on," I said. "You can ride Pete with me."

We walked over to Pete, who looked confused, but seemed to sense the crisis had passed.

"Hello, Pete," I said, and gave him a big hug around the neck. "You're getting both of us for a short trip here. I'll get on first," I said to B.B., "then you get behind."

When we got back to the group they were all sitting on the ground under this big maple tree. Chic was doing magic tricks, scarves in collapsible tubes, disappearing coins and stuff like that. Larry and everyone was watching and laughing except for Pigway and the horses. The horses were tied to trees nearby, eating grass, and Pigway was off somewhere by himself, stuffing his face with organic apricots. He told me that he once ate seventeen Milky Ways without stopping or throwing up. Gross.

So we got back and I helped B.B. down off Pete and we went over to the others.

"Come and join us," said Larry. "Chic is doing some wonderful tricks." He held his arm out to B.B. and she went over and sat next to him. Pretty soon Chic did this trick where he pulled a Styrofoam chicken out of Tuffy Tracktenburg's ear. That made B.B. smile.

After the ride B.B. went to get a carrot for Butterscotch and I took the pills back to Betty Marie. Then I went to Hollow House and wrote another letter to Penny.

Dear Penny,

About three months ago I wrote you a letter asking you to let me know about James. What happened? Did you get my letter? Please, write and let me know. Please, tell me if he's all right. My address is North Woods School, Lake Bomoseen, Vermont.

Thank you.

Love,
Thelma

P.S. Please, answer right away.

I was exhausted. The whole thing with B.B. had really taken it out of me. She was tired too, and we lay around for a while listening to records. Then I fell asleep and had a nightmare, an afternoonmare, really. It was all about having to get to Boston and going up in a plane that didn't have any wings. Nobody knew it didn't have any wings though, and they sent me out to walk on the wing and see why the plane wasn't flying right. I started out and saw that there were no wings, only penguins. Just then B.B. woke me for dinner.

CHAPTER FOURTEEN

I'm looking at this page and I'm realizing that I'm virtually (as in virtuous?) finished with this story. I mean there's me, of course, and the rest of my life, but I can't write about that until it happens unless I want to make it up. It's June now and the academic part of school is ended until September, but in schools like this you don't go home for the summer (thank God!). It's more like summer camp with chores and stuff, and your wonderful therapy sessions, etc., thrown in for good measure.

What's going on now? Riding. We have a horse show this week. It will be my first one. I expect Muffin to win everything, which is all right but embarrassing because of her size and age. I expect to come in second, but I'm looking forward to it no matter what happens. I get to ride Pete which is the main thing I care about.

I can't believe I've worked my way to the end of this. I must thank you, Dr. Stone, for getting me to write. I love it, truly. Also, I must show you this sometime. You deserve a look, wouldn't you say? You've helped me. I have to say it. Painful as my time is with you, I think it's helping. Also, I must thank you for encouraging me to meditate. (This sounds like an Academy Award acceptance speech.) (When is Alan Arkin getting the Oscar he deserves?) Anyway, thank you, Dr. Stone, for your encouragement. I meditate almost every day now, sometimes twice. A lot of times it makes me feel connected with things, like I'm a channel for life the way I feel in those special moments, riding, or looking at the stars. I feel connected with things of the universe that were always inside me, but I had them covered up. I feel it's all one. Not big things and little things or important things and stupid things so much as things connected, or separated. B.B. would know what I mean. Things shut off in boxes, separate from other things, thoughts, feelings. There's trouble (right, Dr. Stone?). Anyway, thank you. I thought your rational mind would mistrust such flights of fancy, but bless you, that's not the case. You're respectful and open-minded and curious and I love you for that.

What else? Peter Westmiller. Our rendezvous at the marshmallow roast was as far as things have gone SO FAR. I hope and pray one day he wakes up and discovers the swan that lurks beneath this stringy-haired juvenile troll and whisks me off to Rutland for a night of passion at the Holiday Inn. Do I really? YES! Well, that and the MAJOR FANTASY. This is really what I want. I run the scene through my mind before sleep each night. The marshmallow roast was wearing a bit thin.

Scene: Peter and me under a tree. One beautiful tree in a large meadow. It's spring, like now. We are fully clothed, he in slacks and V-necked sweater, me in my jeans and green crew neck. He lies back, his head resting on a tree root. I lie back, my head on his chest. He strokes my hair from my forehead straight back. We say nothing for a long time. Then as he strokes my hair he says, "You know, I want to tell you something. I'm very much in love with you. I'm also very much too old for you now, but that won't be true forever. I'll wait for you to grow up." Heaven.

B.B. ran away. We had no idea where she was for five days. The police found her in Virginia (why Virginia?) and I think she's been sent to another school somewhere. I hope they don't lock her up. I was really upset about it. Ever since that day under the tree I feel tied to her in a special way. I asked Larry if she would be all right and he said everybody has to search in their own way. He said the truth can be found anywhere, even in Virginia.

My new roommate is not spectacular, but I've heard that's just as well. They say it's not good to have a real deep relationship with your roommate. They say that causes fights and scenes and that takes a lot of energy, but I'm not sure that's a bad thing. The best roommate is supposed to be someone who doesn't grate on your nerves, but not necessarily one you have a great deal in common with. It's supposed to be simpler. I don't know. Puffy (my new roommate —rhymes with Tuffy) would fall into that category, but she's so bland as to be boring and how can that be good?

Today Muffin and her little brother, Michael, got a hamster. His name is Nibbler. He smells awful, but he's cute. He stays in one of the bathrooms in a Habitrail setup, a plastic apartment complex for rodents, and stuffs food in his cheeks and sits on his plastic exercise disc with his cheeks all puffed out, staring at the shower curtain. God works in mysterious ways.

To keep you up to date before signing off, I have heard

nothing from Penny, also nothing from Jennifer or Kevin and little from my parents, which is fine. My parents may come up to visit in July. I wonder how that will go. This summer I'll be working at the stable full time taking care of the horses and Sachs, the donkey. I rode him last week and is he ever bony! Bony and stubborn!

It's funny, I've left what supposedly is my home, but I feel like I'm really going home. Is that clear? It's like that song that always used to make me cry, "The Sloop *John B.*" It's all about how this sailor wants to go home. It's a folk song. Whenever I heard it, at school, or on T.V. once, I would always cry and feel like I wanted to go home, but the thing was that I always was home, or so I thought. Now I think of home as being inside the knowledge of my own soul. Like that's where I came from. Larry didn't tell me this, it's just stuff I've been coming to. I shared it with him last week during a game of Crazy Eights. It's his favorite game, isn't that strange? About the only thing my father and I enjoyed doing together. No wonder I love it. Larry and I have some great games. I learned more from him playing cards, just playing the game, I mean, without even talking, than from a seminar of lectures by all the other teachers I've ever had put together. What a ghastly thought! Not Mr. Bardenias who was always lowering and raising the window pole and dropping his glasses and forgetting his place midway through an equation! Not Miss McTrevin with the rattly dentures and the desk full of Certs ("be certain"). Anyway, I've had some good teachers, especially up here, but a card game with Larry wins hands down. I can see my work with Larry as a never-ending thing. I mean I'll leave here (eventually, I expect), but I feel that Larry will still be my teacher. It will be interesting to see how that works.

Anyway, we were playing Crazy Eights in the rec room by the fire. I had stopped writing for a while and he was playing with some other kid. I think it was Chic, but I'm not sure. Anyway, he was playing with somebody else and I stopped writing and asked if I could join them. Yes, it was Chic. I remember he had his muffler on, even by the fire. Larry said sure and Chic said he had to write a letter to his mother so Larry and I started a game.

"I was thinking," I said, after we'd been playing for a while.

"Yes?"

"About what life is like to me sometimes."

"What's that? Clubs." He put down an eight of hearts and called it clubs. You can make eights any suit you want.

"I was thinking that life is sort of like a costume party."

"You think so?"

"Sometimes."

I had to draw a card. The suit was still clubs and I didn't have any.

"You got one!" said Larry. "Good for you!"

He gets just as excited when I win as when he wins. He loves it all.

"Life seems like this costume party where everyone comes and then they forget it's a party and they forget to leave. They think they really are who they came as. Like if I came as Peter Pan or Captain Hook I'd just forget after a while and think I really was them and if somebody told me I wasn't I'd yell at them and get mad. I'd drink all this punch and have these cookies and stuff and dance and get compliments on my costume and I'd forget that there had been anything before that. Does this make sense?"

"Indeed."

"I'm glad."

"Right to the heart of the matter. Last card." You have to tell when you have only one card left.

"I mean you have to believe in continuing soul experience to buy my image."

"Do *you*?"

"I think so. It would be like each lifetime as a certain personality is your costume. Going home would be leaving the party. Do you have to die to do that?"

"Not at all. You go home on the inside. You can be anywhere. Yogis can do this while still in the body. You can do it. It takes work."

"I'd like to know who I am inside my costume. Then I could stay at the party and have punch and cookies and dance with a strong sense and memory of who I am and where I came from and what I'm doing at the party in the first place. That's what I'd like to do."

"You can. I'm out."

"You won?"

"Out on a diamond. Want to play again?"

"Sure."

"Margaret said once a long time ago, well a few months ago, that she developed this passion for discovering what's true. I feel that way. Like I heard a funny thing yesterday."

"What was that?"

"You know Muffin's little brother, Michael?"

"Yes."

"Well, I heard him talking with Muffin in the kitchen. He said, 'Where did the earth come from?' and Muffin said, 'It came from outer space' and Michael said, 'O.K., but where did outer space come from?' "

"What do you make of that? Hearts." He had changed his eight of spades to a heart.

"I don't know. I bet there is an answer although scientists don't know it yet."

"I don't have any more hearts."

"Is there?"

"What?"

"Is there an answer?"

"To the origin of outer space?"

"Yes."

"Sure."

"Where did it come from?"

"You can know that. The answer will come from the inside. That's the only way it will have any meaning. You already know all there is to know."

"I just don't know it yet."

"Right."

It came!!! I just heard from Penny and cried all over the letter.

Here it is:

> *Dear Thelma,*
>
> *I'm sorry, but I never got your letter. Ronald must have shredded it for the guinea pig's cage or something because I never even knew about it.*
>
> *Now about James. The day after you left I saw him in the garage and he looked really sad so I rang your parents' bell and asked your mother if I*

could take him over to my house to play. She said yes so that's what I did. Now every day after school we bring him over to our house. On the weekends he stays all day. When I have to baby-sit and can't get him Sam does it. James loves it up here. We wrestle and he chases sticks and does all kinds of stuff. He loves chocolate grahams. We give him one every day or an oatmeal cookie or something else my mom bakes. Don't worry. He's doing great. Take care. See ya.

Love,
Penny

I couldn't stop crying. I was standing in the hallway outside the dining room and it was almost lunchtime. Kids were everywhere, screaming and running around, paying no attention to me standing in the corner with my letter. JAMES! MY DARLING JAMES! ALIVE! I LOVE YOU! I read the letter over and over again and cried and cried. Larry was standing by the bulletin board and he looked over at me and smiled. He knew how happy I was.